FICTION

The
Stolen
Heart

ALSO BY LAUREN KELLY

Take Me, Take Me with You

The Stolen Heart

A Novel of Suspense

LAUREN KELLY

ecco

An Imprint of HarperCollinsPublishers

An excerpt from part I appeared in *The Harvard Review*, spring 2005.

Meal preparations in several chapters are derived from recipes in *The Good Food* by Daniel Halpern and Julie Strand.

THE STOLEN HEART. Copyright © 2005 by The Ontario Review, Inc. All rights reserved. Printed in the United States of America. No part of this book may be used or reproduced in any manner whatsoever without written permission except in the case of brief quotations embodied in critical articles and reviews. For information, address HarperCollins Publishers Inc., 10 East 53rd Street, New York, NY 10022.

HarperCollins books may be purchased for educational, business, or sales promotional use. For information, please write: Special Markets Department, HarperCollins Publishers Inc., 10 East 53rd Street, New York, NY 10022.

FIRST EDITION

Designed by Joseph Rutt

Library of Congress Cataloging-in-Publication Data has been applied for.

ISBN 0-06-079728-2

04   05   06   07   WBC/RRDH   10   9   8   7   6   5   4   3   2   1

To Janet Hutchings

I

Taken

She'd been taken it was said.

Not said aloud! Not in our hearing.

But if you listened. If you listened hard. If you listened past the scared sound of your heart beating. That low rumbling sound like thunder. *Taken!*

A girl had been taken. From Highlands Park. I knew where that was. I knew who the girl was. We were not supposed to know, yet. We were too young to know. We were very quiet, we did not want to be taken, too. The girl who'd been taken had not been a quiet girl but giggly and squirmy and unpredictable in her behavior. I saw a giant bird descending from the sky to punish her. I saw the sky darken with the giant bird's outspread wings and bared talons and I saw Lilac Jimson seized in those talons and lifted screaming into the sky.

Taken where?

It was May 1988. I was ten years old. I was in fifth grade at Thomas Jefferson Elementary. I was not a close friend of Lilac Jimson. I saw Lilac running with her brother Roosevelt after school. Roosevelt was older than Lilac, and taller. And Lilac was a year older than me but not taller. Different cleaning ladies came to our house on Lincoln Avenue and one of them used to be Lilac's mother who was called Alina and who spoke in a strange way, it was hard to understand. When someone said *That little gypsy-looking girl* it was Lilac Jimson they meant. *That little colored girl with the tooth.* Because Lilac had a gold tooth that flashed when she smiled. Lilac had tight-braided dark hair and skin like creamy cocoa and beautiful sparkly-black eyes. I wanted to be Lilac Jimson's friend but there was some strangeness between us, Lilac laughed and smiled at everybody but not at me. Lilac's sparkly eyes just jumped over me like I wasn't there. I was hurt, I didn't understand. Maybe it had to do with Lilac's mother who'd used to clean our house but now another woman, a black woman, cleaned our house. Maybe Lilac's mother had told her not to like me because I was Mr. Graf's daughter and because I lived in that big cobblestone house on Lincoln Avenue with all the trees. I wanted to invite Lilac home with me but I knew that Lilac would laugh and turn away without hearing me. Lilac was so pretty!— the only girl who could climb the ropes in gym class, like a little monkey, to the ceiling. Lilac was the first girl at Thomas Jefferson Elementary to get pierced ears, when she was ten. Lilac was a girl to be scolded for being "wiggly" in her desk but our teacher laughed saying this, you could see Miss Hansen liked Lilac Jimson. But now suddenly Lilac Jimson was *That poor little girl who was taken from the park nobody knows where maybe in the river the latest is police are questioning her own father isn't that tragic.*

The Glass Heart

—

It was a sculpted-glass heart I'd given my father, that was taken from him when he was dying.

It was a beautiful sculpted-glass heart but not very large.

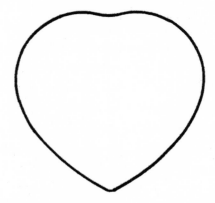

I purchased the glass heart in a store on Madison Avenue, New York City. A store of glittering glass objects, mostly imports. I had not much money of my own but this was such a beautiful piece of sculpted glass, with powers of magnification as well, I had to buy it. I was not thinking at the time *Why am I buying a glass heart to give to my father* for it was the beauty of the object that drew my attention, and the attention of my companion.

The glass heart was marked VENEZIA on its underside.

The glass heart weighed heavy and snug in the palm of my hand.

The glass heart absorbed the warmth of my hand, the beat of my blood, with surprising boldness. I smiled, in surprise. For shouldn't glass be *cold*?

My companion, with whom I'd been traveling for a brief, intense period in my life, shortly to end, wanted to buy the glass heart for me but quickly I told him no, I wanted to buy the glass heart for myself.

"There's someone I want to give it to. I want it only for him."

Gifts you give out of love. Gifts you give out of the sickest guilt. This gift to my father of the sculpted-glass heart was both.

"Well, Merilee. What's this?"

My father was suspicious of gifts. Even within the family. He had an aristocrat's soul that is offended by the pushy aggression of gift-giving.

Especially, Daddy had never appreciated gifts intended to bear some intimate message.

In this case, the sculpted-glass heart seemed to be intended as a reading aid for Dennis Graf's aging eyes. Yes?

Daddy didn't ask. I hadn't said so. The fact that the glass heart was also a magnifying glass was secondary to its beauty, I might have argued.

" 'Venezia.' Did you buy it there?"

I told Daddy no. I'd bought it in New York City.

(As if I might have traveled to Venice without informing my father. As if my life had become so clandestine, so beyond his radar.)

Relations between us had long been uneasy, strained. I had moved away from Mt. Olive permanently. I had attended a small liberal arts college without exactly graduating. I had insisted upon living "my own" life elsewhere and it wasn't clear to my father what sort of life I was living, who my companions were and why I'd never brought one of them home to Mt. Olive to introduce to him. *He knows that I have a sexual life. Yet he can't bear it, he no longer has a sexual life of his own.*

My mother had died four years ago. Since then, my father had begun to age, visibly. And in his behavior, his habits. He'd sold his successful import business and was now more or less retired. He'd dropped out of an active role in local politics. (He'd served two terms on the Mt. Olive city council and as mayor of the small city of 35,000 inhabitants in the Chautauqua Valley east of Port Oriskany.) His public interests now were mainly philanthropic, the kind executed by donations and endowments arranged by lawyers. I had the uneasy feeling speaking with Daddy on the phone (our calls had always been infrequent, and uneasy) that he was spending more and more time alone. He had a housekeeper, and he had a "trusted assistant" who dealt with money matters, but he seemed to have given up an active social life. When I'd last visited I noticed how he blinked and stared and squinted through his bifocal glasses, with a look of impotent fury, bringing printed material grudgingly into the light to see it more clearly. But, being Daddy, he'd only just laughed when I suggested that he see an eye doctor and get his prescription changed.

As if to say *Why the hell bother? I'm an old man.*

But you aren't an old man! I wanted to protest. At the time, Daddy was only seventy-one.

My mother's death had been a shock to him, I had to suppose. He had found her collapsed in an upstairs bathroom. Only just fifty-one, she'd died of a stroke. At the time I'd been nineteen and somewhat estranged from both my parents.

Daddy how could this happen   how could Mom die

I mean, how could Mom who wasn't old   die

Wasn't there any warning   did she have headaches

What were my mother's last words

Questions I did not ask. Not then, and not afterward.

"So! 'Venezia.' Who did you travel with, Merilee, to the beautiful doomed city on the sea?"

I wondered if Daddy was testing me. Teasing me. Hoping to trip me up in a lie.

I smiled, and repeated that I hadn't bought the glass heart in Venice, but in New York City. I'd seen it, and thought of him; and impulsively bought it. That was all.

The way my father held the sculpted-glass heart in the palm of his hand made me wonder if he was thinking of my mother. Poor Edith! Maybe Daddy felt some tinge of guilt, regret. He had not been what you'd have called an attentive husband. An affectionate husband. (A faithful husband?) But now the large old cobblestone house at 299 Lincoln Avenue felt like a mausoleum. Daddy never entertained any longer, lived in just a few rooms of the house and had shut up the rest. A housekeeper came several times a week to maintain the house and to prepare meals, if Daddy wasn't eating out.

Aging but not-yet-old. Staring into the sculpted-glass heart as if staring into his own (clouded?) future.

We were in Daddy's study. Where for years I'd been allowed to come only at Daddy's invitation.

It was a beautiful room grown slightly shabby. The heavy Chinese carpet needed hand-cleaning, the dusty brocaded drapes needed replacing. The tall leaded-glass windows needed cleaning inside and out. Daddy's furnishings in this room were Victorian-gentlemen's-club: mahogany and leather, stolid, stumpy, impressive. That special leather-smell I would associate all my life with my father's study and what a privilege it was when he'd invited me inside to visit with him.

I wanted to think that Dennis Graf was still a vigorous, handsome man. Though his eyes were pouched in loose flesh like a turtle's and his skin was creased as if with a netting of cobwebs. Though his manner was more distracted, preoccupied. He seemed to be stirred by, or maybe just annoyed by, the word *Venezia,* which might have triggered a disturbing memory. I knew that Daddy had traveled to Venice years ago, more than once. While I'd been growing up he was often away on business trips to southern Europe, northern Africa, Turkey, the Far East. Graf Imports, Inc. had specialized in importing high-quality goods: works of art, handwoven tapestries, perfumes, spices, upscale gifts of all kinds. Traveling, Daddy had usually taken with him a younger Graf relative who'd served as his chief accountant, assistant, and companion. He'd never taken his family with him. He had not taken my mother with him, not once.

Was this strange? I hadn't thought so, at the time. Growing up as Dennis Graf's daughter I wasn't likely to have judged him.

In this study and scattered through the house were memen-
tos from Daddy's many trips. Stone figures, wall tapestries, beautifully dyed shawls draped across tables, handwoven carpets. On
the floor-to-ceiling shelves in the study were countless travel
books. Many of these were oversized and nearly too heavy to lift.
There were books of exotic photographs, elaborate maps both
current and historic. My father was the only person I'd ever met
who owned one of those large fantastically detailed globes of the
earth which you turn with your fingers, attached to a handsome
carved-mahogany base, the sort of thing seen usually in refer-
ence rooms of older, affluent public libraries.

This globe was close beside Daddy's desk where, turning in
his swivel chair, he could idly rotate it, in a contemplative mood.
I saw that it was still in perfect condition, after decades. When
I'd been a naive little girl I had imagined that Earth was colored
like Daddy's globe, each country marked off from its neighbors
by a distinctive color and a thin black outline.

Daddy had acquired the globe in the 1950s. Many, perhaps
most of the countries indicated on its surface no longer existed.
Their names had been changed. Their territories. Entire cultures
had been wiped away. The melancholy thought came to me that
when my father died, the beautiful globe would be taken away as
trash.

To break the awkward silence, I suggested that Daddy use the
glass heart to read maps. "Some of your maps, Daddy, the print is
so small it's impossible to . . ."

Daddy made a sucking noise with his lips. One of his old-
man habits, that had emerged in the past year or so. A veiled
look came over his face. He didn't like anyone, especially one of

the women in his family, to tell him what to do, even elliptically. I worried that he'd open his fingers (as if accidentally) and the heart would fall to the hardwood floor where it would shatter with a sound like sharp staccato laughter.

Instead, Daddy tossed the sculpted-glass heart in his hand. As if it weren't exquisite, expensive. As if it were a tennis ball, an orange. Tossed it, caught it, saw the look of fleeting alarm in my face, and winked at me. "Well, Merilee! You've become quite the gift-giver, eh?"

Was this an accusation, or some sort of chiding praise! I waited for Daddy to say more. Trying to smile, leaning forward in anticipation.

Not until nearly two years later in June 2004 would I see the sculpted-glass heart again, locating it in my father's study to bring to him in the cardiac unit of Mt. Olive General Hospital.

Gift-Giver

*Q*uite the gift-giver. You've become.
   Well, Merilee!

He'd meant to mock, I think. Or maybe it was an expression of sympathy. *Gift-giver: my daughter.*

I knew exactly how it had begun, and when.

". . . hearing about it soon enough, Edith. If you don't want to tell the child, I will."

My aunt was talking to my mother. My aunt had a way of speaking like knife blades chopping and my mother's voice was doughy-soft like bread.

". . . called and asked me to drop by. He's concerned about Merilee, and he's concerned about you. 'Tell Edith there's no danger for *us.*' He's going to post a reward, if the little girl isn't found by tonight. He's going to join the search team, if . . ."

At this time, Lilac Jimson had been missing for more than forty hours. It was late afternoon of the day following the day following the evening of May 22, 1988, when Lilac Jimson had been taken, it was believed from a picnic grove above a steep, treacherous-rocky ravine that ran through Highlands Park.

I knew none of this. I was a child who could not have said the date of any day. I was considered a bright child in school and yet probably I could not have said, without pausing to think hard, the name of the month, even the date of the year.

Facts are obdurate as rocks, boulders. Facts are the province of adults. Children's eyes are drawn to balloons, floating things.

Facts haven't much meaning to children. Only when they cease to be children.

This fact: of the (white, well-to-do) residents of the Lincoln Avenue section of Mt. Olive, my father Dennis Graf, at this time a former mayor of Mt. Olive, in his late fifties and still an active civic leader, was one of the few to involve himself in the search for eleven-year-old Lilac Jimson. When a $20,000 reward was of-fered for information leading to the return of Lilac Jimson, or-ganized by a "coalition of concerned Mt. Olive citizens," as the local media would report, most of the $20,000 had been pledged by Dennis Graf.

So I would learn, eventually. Though not from my father who was, in unexpected ways, considering his gregarious personality, a reticent man who shrank from seeming to speak well of himself.

". . . really, Edith! We are quite safe *here.* Merilee should re-turn to school tomorrow. You don't want to make her fearful and anxious . . ."

Fearful and anxious like you.

The women were in the kitchen. The door was shut. My mother and my aunt probably thought that I was upstairs in my room for I'd been "sick with fever" that morning. I'd crept down the stairs slowly, knowing precisely which steps creaked, and where. My caution wasn't so very different from the caution of my game of coming down these stairs stepping only on the insides of the steps and never on the carpet where, if you stared hard, you could see dark squiggly shapes like snakes.

There was a front staircase in our house, with a plush dark-rose carpet and no snakes. It was only the back stairs leading down to the kitchen and the back hall where, in the dark-patterned carpet, the snakes hid.

No time for snakes now! I was listening to my aunt Cameron talking to my mother. "Eavesdropping" in practice before I knew the terminology, or even the concept. "Eavesdropping" in order to hear what I was not supposed to hear and so it was crucial, I couldn't let them see me.

Merilee! my mother would cry in a thin hurt wail of a voice which was a signal of my mother's anger always kept hidden in the way my mother wore loose-fitting slope-shouldered cardigan sweaters over shirts and loose-fitting baggy slacks to hide her stick-body inside.

Merilee what are you doing, you bad girl what are you thinking my mother would cry breathless and wounded and tears would well in her red-rimmed eyes and make me ashamed.

When Aunt Cameron came to our house and Daddy wasn't home it was for a purpose. For Aunt Cameron would not come to visit my mother without a purpose. You could hear in Aunt Cameron's voice how she was trying to be patient with my mother the way our teacher Miss Hansen tried to be patient with certain of my classmates for whom reading and arithmetic did not come easily. It was a Graf way of speaking. It was Daddy's way of speaking he sometimes softened with a wink and a smile.

"... that little gypsy-looking girl, is it? Her mother used to clean house here ..."

My heart began to beat hard, I gripped my knees tight against my chest. I knew it was Lilac Jimson my aunt meant.

"... from Poland, couldn't speak English very well, poor thing. And taking up with that big hulking black man from the West Indies, that got fired from his janitor-job, I heard, 'way back last winter and hasn't been working since. It isn't surprising that something terrible has happened, seven children living in that row house, you have to wonder what goes on in households like that, this wasn't on the local news but people are saying there may be drugs involved, a drug dealer from Rochester, black of course, the poor little girl might have been taken for revenge and her own father might be involved, the police have been questioning him I've heard, including Rochester police, Dennis said he hoped to God that this wasn't it, those people can be vicious to one another ..." My aunt's chop-chopping voice paused, my mother might have murmured a response, or nodded her head, the way my mother had learned to do at such times knowing that some sort of response was required to indicate that she was listening. And Aunt Cameron continued, vehement as a scolding schoolteacher, "... imagine, seven children in that family! And all of them dark like gypsies. People are saying that the little girl who was taken is very pretty, a bright lively little girl, still you have to wonder, exactly what was she doing wandering off from her sisters, the poor child I can only imagine how terrified, well I can't imagine, it's so awful. You know they say, if a child is taken and isn't found within twenty-four hours, or if the kidnapper doesn't call . . ." Aunt Cameron sighed loudly. There was a scraping of her chair against the tile floor of the kitchen, like punctuation. "One of the stories I'd heard was her sisters hadn't missed her, at the park? Where there was some kind of game? Mostly older black boys, I think. Of course they are all being questioned. And the father. And the mother. Oh that poor woman, that poor pathetic woman just think what she must be living through, her daughter missing and she must blame herself, she should blame herself, being involved with such . . . Well!" My aunt's voice dipped in indignation, then resurfaced crackling with reproach. "The sisters hadn't even missed her, at the park. And it was after dark. They thought she'd already gone home, they said. You have to wonder if those young girls were drinking, or smoking dope, or worse. Of course they were fooling around with boys. Probably adult men! They get themselves pregnant already in middle school, those 'coloreds.' And with a mother like that . . ."—my aunt made a harsh sound as if she was clearing her nose, in disgust—". . . can't be expected to behave any differently, I suppose. We are so lucky in Mt. Olive that we don't have much of this. Just along Eastman and South Main. And that block of row houses by the train depot. The county welfare office has much to answer for, giving financial support to people like that! I know, some of them work. This 'Alina' works. But she still had time to take up housekeeping with this man named 'Jimson' didn't she! How a woman from Warsaw who can't speak English, who people say isn't 'right in the head,' takes up with a black man, I can't imagine, can you? Maybe in a tavern? I only hope, Edith, that when she worked in this house she didn't bring the little girl along and Merilee never met the child . . ."

I waited for my mother to say yes Merilee has met her. Merilee knows Lilac Jimson, they are in the same grade at school.

But Mom said nothing, that I could hear. I had to imagine her fretful and frowning, not wishing to risk an opinion. In Aunt Cameron's presence, as in Daddy's, my mother was very quiet. Words that seemed to tumble with such ease and authority from other's mouths were stopped-up and choked in hers.

"... I realize, they attend the same school. But Merilee doesn't associate with such girls, does she? Dennis says he doesn't think so. He says it has been at least three years since this 'Alina' worked for you, and so . . ."

Three years. If Daddy said so, it was so. But I seemed to remember Lilac's mother Alina, not so long ago. She was a short fattish white-skinned woman with a voice that chattered at you, like a bird chirping. She wore coveralls and tied her straw-colored hair back in a scarf. Cleaning house, she hummed and sang with the noise of the vacuum cleaner. She called me what sounded like "Mary Leigh" and said I had the prettiest curls she'd ever seen.

More than once, Alina brought Lilac to our house. But Lilac had to stay in the kitchen, to wait for Alina to finish her work. I would catch a glimpse of her, *the little gypsy-looking girl* as my mother called her, but I wasn't allowed to play with her. Mostly when cleaning women came to the house, Mom left to go shopping and took me with her. Strangers in the house made her nervous, she said. She felt bad, other women working for *her*. Before marrying my father, she'd worked. Oh she'd worked from the time she was fifteen—my mother began to tell me, then thought better of it.

Aunt Cameron's voice was lifting now, roused as if to action. ". . . better for us to tell her, Edith, than for her to hear of it from other children. I only pray, if that poor child has been taken by some sex maniac and murdered, it happened far away, and her body is never found. The very worst that can happen, the worst nightmare for Mt. Olive, is that she is found somewhere close by, and . . ."

I was crouched on the stairs, hugging my knees to my chest. I felt an icy wave wash over me. I'd heard my aunt's terrible words and yet I had not. I'd heard the mix of alarm and petulance in her voice but I couldn't make sense of her words.

Taken. Sex maniac. Murdered.

That morning my mother hadn't wanted me to go to school. Touching my forehead with her cold fingers saying I had a fever, no no *no* I was not going to school. It was raining, it was a dark day, *no.* I would have to stay home, in bed.

I saw the worry in my mother's eyes, that scared me. In my confusion I thought maybe what had happened to Lilac Jimson was beginning to happen to me.

Already I felt sickish, weak. My mouth was dry like sand. My skin smarted where the sheets touched it.

The day before at school there was Lilac's empty desk. Right there at the front of the room, farthest row to the right by the windows. Lilac was so squirmy and wiggly, Miss Hansen said she wanted Lilac to sit "right where I can see you." Miss Hansen liked Lilac, though. You could see that Miss Hansen liked Lilac a lot though Lilac was restless when we were doing arithmetic and had a way of twisting in her desk, to laugh over her shoulder at her friends. Her smile had a flash of gold. The tiny studs in her ears were gold. Her eyes were sparkly-black like my favorite doll's eyes except those eyes would never look at me, and I could not ask why.

But already at school there was talk, something had happened to Lilac Jimson which was why she wasn't in school, something had happened that wasn't just being sick or falling off a bicycle and hurting herself, it had happened in Highlands Park only a mile away from Thomas Jefferson Elementary, Lilac had been *taken,* Lilac was *missing* and nobody knew where. All day, Miss Hansen was nervous and distracted glancing often at the door as if expecting someone to come in, but no one did. Not once did Miss Hansen comment on Lilac's vacant desk right in front of her and not once did any of us ask about Lilac. Most of us were sitting stiff and strange at our desks. Nobody talked much. Only a few boys acted silly. But even these boys didn't dare ask about Lilac Jimson.

I knew not to ask about her. Not at school, and not at home.

Usually I walked home from school, but that day Mom was parked at the curb to take me home. I knew from the nervous way she smiled and didn't ask anything about school that I wasn't supposed to know the little I knew about Lilac and that, if my mother suspected that I knew even the little that I knew, she would be upset. And Daddy would be disgusted with her, for Daddy didn't like Mom when she was being what he called *anxious, nerved-up.*

What he called *weak-minded* and *unstable* and *not a healthy influence on our daughter.*

". . . can't be shielded. It will only make her more . . ."

Chairs were being scraped against the kitchen floor. I had to escape, I knew that my mother would come looking for me. If

I went back upstairs to my room I'd be trapped. I knew how my mother's thin wavering voice would lift up the stairs—"Merilee? Are you there?" I slipped outside through the back door. The rain had stopped, there was bright blinding sunshine. Like other properties on Lincoln Avenue ours was so large you could hardly see to the end of it. There were many places where I could hide: behind the garage, behind the gardening sheds, in the old pear orchard. I knew a secret place at the very back where I could crawl through an evergreen hedge and hide down in the ravine about a hundred feet away, a deep rocky gorge where I wasn't supposed to play because I might hurt myself, except I knew that this was the same ravine that ran through Highlands Park.

Close behind the house was a swing set. I ran there, and began swinging. I wasn't hiding, Mom could find me. I didn't want not to be found. Gripping the rope handles tight and pushing myself into the air. Shut my eyes tight kicking both feet hard against the ground. Higher, higher! Thinking *Until Mom tells me about Lilac it hasn't happened yet*. At a short distance I could hear my mother's plaintive voice—"Merilee? Where are you?" My eyes were shut but I could see my mother's tense worried face, that looked like a girl's face until you came closer.

"Merilee for heaven's sake! I have something to tell you, please stop that swinging."

I opened my eyes. It was Aunt Cameron, not Mom.

Now it was too late to hide. For Lilac Jimson, and for me.

Next day, it began.

I mean, I began. "Gift-giving."

I don't remember where the idea came from. I don't remember having any clear motives for anything I did as a child. But I began to take to school certain of my "treasures" and gave them to girls who were friends or almost-friends or girls I hoped would be my friends. If Lilac Jimson had been in school I would have given her my nicest treasure, a pink "real pearl" necklace my grandmother Graf had given to me for "when Merilee is older."

There was also a silver pin I loved, in the shape of a kitty-cat with tiny blue sapphires for eyes. There was an American Princess Barbie Doll with a tiara and a white taffeta gown, and there was a plastic sphere with a large beautiful black and yellow butterfly inside, kept on a windowsill in my room. There was an almost-new watercolor set, and there was my special silver spoon with the initial *M* engraved on the handle, and there were books, my favorite Black Stallion books. All of these I gave away. (The silver spoon, I gave to a shy girl named Miranda who almost cried to think that I'd bought a spoon with *M* engraved on it just for her.) I was so nice, I was the nicest girl in fifth grade. I was so generous, I was like a flash fire throwing off sparks and light! I made new friends, and girls who'd already been my friends liked me better.

Six school days in a row, and Lilac Jimson was still missing.

I would have said that the treasures were mine to give away because they were mine but I hid them from my mother, who drove me to school every day now, and picked me up after school. And so I must have known that what I was doing was "bad." I must have known that my parents would not like what I was doing. Yet my ten-year-old's logic was if my parents did not know what I was doing, it could not be "bad."

On the seventh day, Miss Hansen began to be suspicious of

me. For always there was a flurry of activity around me, with my new friends. And there were girls eager to be my friends, even boys were crowding around me. Miss Hansen took me aside and asked what I was doing and the girl to whom I was giving one of my treasures quickly pushed it back at me and said she didn't want it. And Miss Hansen said, "Oh Merilee," in a sad voice, but did not scold me. But when Mom came to pick me up that afternoon she was close to crying, for Miss Hansen had called to tell her what I'd done. Mom had searched my room and discovered things missing. One of these, the pink pearl necklace, she called a "family heirloom." I tried to explain that the treasures were mine to give away but Mom was agitated as I'd rarely seen her saying I had no right, I had no right to give my possessions away, especially the pearl necklace from Grandmother Graf I'd never yet been allowed to wear. "If your father finds out, he will be furious at both of us."

My mother's face was sickly-white splotched with freckles like discolored raindrops. I was embarrassed of her in public for she seemed so unlike the mothers of my classmates, her eyes downcast and her manner edgy and apologetic. If someone said, "Hello, Mrs. Graf," she reacted with a nervous smile and barely murmured a response. My father disliked my mother looking "washed-out" and "plain" in public so whenever Mom left the house she hastily smeared crimson lipstick on her mouth, but wore no other makeup and only just brushed her sparrow-colored hair back behind her ears. She was tall, nearly six feet. She carried herself with an oddly aggressive shyness. Her mouth had a look of rubbery anguish as if, instead of smiling, her mouth really wanted to cry. Her eyes had a look of hot, pent-up tears as if, even when she was smiling, her eyes really wanted to cry. In my mother's large-knuckled hands there was a perpetual tremor as if those hands really wanted to close into fists and strike out. (In fact, Mom never struck me, never even squeezed my arm or shoulder to discipline me. Her admonitions were all verbal, sighs and sobs. I saw with surprise how the mothers of other children stooped to hug and kiss them, and the children hugged and kissed their mothers, as if this was the most natural behavior in the world!)

My mother did not touch me now, though her hands trembled. She was short of breath, struggling to speak.

"Merilee. How could you . . ."

Now I began to cry. Now I was more frightened for myself than for Lilac Jimson.

I was made to understand that I'd done something very bad. And that my mother would try to protect me, from my father finding out.

Of the treasures I'd given away, that I had to confess to Mom, the "heirloom" necklace of pink pearls and the silver spoon engraved with my initial and the beautiful big black and yellow butterfly (that my father had brought back to me from a faraway exotic country called Thailand) were most important. Mom wrote notes to the mothers of the girls to whom I'd given these gifts, for Mom hated to use the telephone, and within a few days all three gifts were returned through the mail.

So ashamed! A gift-giver who takes back her gifts.

Daddy never knew what I'd done. Mom and I never spoke of the incident afterward. (As we never spoke of Lilac Jimson and what might have become of her.) I was made to feel embarrassed and ashamed at school and I understood that I must be extra-nice all the time now, to be liked. I would become one of those girls (there were several in fifth grade) who said only nice things about others and not nasty things. I would practice smiling into a mirror. I would become a pretty girl with dark-brown springy hair and dark shining eyes. I would smile to make people like me. Even if they didn't like me, I would smile at them, and eventually they would like me; or, if they didn't, if they distrusted my smile, my wish to believe only the best of people or at any rate to behave as if I believed only the best, it would not matter because to observe me smiling happily you would conclude that Merilee Graf was well liked, she was a good girl with many friends and not the kind of girl to whom anything bad would ever happen, maybe.

"Jim-Jim"

I was a pretty girl, now I'm a pretty woman: twenty-six years old. In pleated cherry-red silk, shimmering. In my shiny-dark springy hair trimmed short, exposing the tips of my ivory ears. I'm quick to smile, it's instinctive. I'm a gift-giver who gives the gift of myself knowing that I can take it back at any time.

At least, that has been my practice. I will have to admit that I've made a few mistakes.

"Hey: Mer'lee."

". . . Roosevelt."

It was a shock. He'd taken me by surprise. Stepping out of the elevator into the lobby of Mt. Olive General Hospital as I was about to step inside. Hardly an hour in Mt. Olive, after a six-hour drive upstate, and one of the first people I see is Roosevelt Jimson. My eyes had been wide open but I hadn't been seeing a thing. My mouth had been shaped in its usual anticipatory half-moon of a smile but my heart had been clenching in dread of what awaited me upstairs in the cardiac unit. And there, looming above me, Roosevelt Jimson's sharp-angled face with that burnt-gingery skin that looked just as I remembered, as if it had been brought to a simmer and about to burst with heat.

"So: how's it going?"

"It . . ."

My voice was weak and wavery. My pretty-girl poise had been knocked from me as if the man had shoved me back with the flat of his big meaty hand. I hadn't seen Roosevelt Jimson in six or seven years. If I'd known who would be stepping off that elevator, I'd have hidden somewhere and waited for him to pass by. Maybe he knew this, the way his eyes held steady on me. For there was what you'd call a history between us.

Why I'd called Jimson by his formal first name, I don't know. I was sure I'd never called him "Roosevelt" before, no one who knew him did. Even as a boy, swaggering and self-confident, he'd been known as "Jimson." I'd registered the disdain in his eyes when I'd stammered "Roosevelt."

Don't try that white-girl shit with me, like you don't know Jimson.

I was being jostled by people getting onto the elevator. Jimson was standing holding the door open for me to step inside but distracted by him I'd lost track of what I was doing. He had asked *how's it going.* I felt something white-hot and dazzling pass over my brain. *How's it going, I think my father is dying.*

". . . not so well, I guess. My father . . ."

"Yeh. I heard."

Jimson's face seemed to darken. He hadn't smiled at me, he'd never been one to be inveigled into smiling just because someone was smiling at him. His eyes were heavy-lidded, the whites oddly lustrous and lightly threaded with blood. He looked like he'd been smoking dope. Or maybe he had a mild buzz on, from a few beers. Back in high school he'd played football for the Mt. Olive team and his nose had been broken. His singed-looking skin, a little darker than Lilac's gypsy-skin, exuded the same odd lustre, so unlike the flat-matte skin of Caucasians like me. As far back as I could remember, when I'd first become conscious of male sexuality, I'd understood that Roosevelt Jimson, forever known in Mt. Olive as an older brother of Lilac Jimson, had played his blackness with white girls like a tenor sax. He'd been a lanky lumbering boy with a mock-gallant manner, a sullen-sexy smile turned on and off like a light; a black boy who'd murmured "Yes'm" and "No*sirr*" to adults with a breathy vehemence that might have been excessively polite, or insolent. Already in high school he'd gotten in various kinds of trouble. Maybe he'd never graduated. In the past few years he'd grown into a hard-muscled man, his head shaved at the sides and back like a fighter's. The lower part of his face was disfigured by a goatee that looked mean as steel wool.

The thought came to me fleeting as a ray of light. How that wiry facial hair would hurt, rubbed against a woman's soft skin.

". . . with the Mt. Olive police, I'd heard? Or is it the county . . ."

But Jimson wasn't in any kind of uniform, he was wearing unpressed khakis and a white T-shirt. A thin gold chain around his neck. He glanced down at himself, laughed and scowled. *Don't go there* was the admonition.

If he'd been a law enforcement officer, he wasn't one now. It was difficult to imagine this man in uniform.

He told me he was visiting a friend in the hospital who'd cracked up his car. Somberly he told me yes, he'd heard that my father was in the hospital, too. "Say h'lo to Mr. Graf for me, okay? Tell him 'Roosevelt Jimson' . . ." His voice trailed off as if he had more to say but was thinking better of it.

I thanked him. I said yes, I would.

I felt a small thrill of pride, that Jimson had spoken of my father in a tone of respect.

He wouldn't mock Dennis Graf, would he? Maybe then he wouldn't mock me.

I'd missed the first elevator. Now the doors to another were opening. I needed to break away from this man with the shaved head and bewhiskered jaws and eyes that slashed like a razor but I heard myself saying, "I remember, Lilac used to call you 'Jim-Jim.' After school we'd see the two of you running along the railroad track, you'd cross the trestle bridge where pedestrians weren't supposed to go and especially . . ."

My voice trailed off. I'd been about to say *especially little girls.*

Jimson's face shut up tight. He didn't want to hear this. He was furious at me for bringing it up. Out of his back pocket he'd pulled a creased baseball cap and fitted it on his head in a gesture of barely controlled rage. He gave me a mock-salute. His lips twitched in a mock-smile. *Girl don't fuck with me: you had your chance.*

Before I could murmur an apology, Jimson was gone.

This was the day, June 11, 2004, when I returned to Mt. Olive, New York, to begin my melancholy vigil at my father's bedside. It was a vigil that would continue for longer than I expected and maybe it's continuing, still.

Ravine Road

. . . that wild lurching drive. Ravine Road where (it was his belief) whoever had taken his sister had been cruising that night. Because Ravine Road bisected the park, in the area in which Lilac might have been walking. Because Ravine Road was unpaved, narrow and not frequently used. Because Ravine Road had no streetlights. Because Ravine Road descended steeply to the plank bridge then rose again in a sequence of tight, blind curves. Because Ravine Road was a lonely road even by day. Because Lilac would have been trailing after her sisters, or maybe on her way home. Right along here, he said. See how there's trees close to the road, like a hiding place for somebody with bad intentions. Seeing a little girl by herself, and almost dark, and . . . His voice was young, raw, quavering. His voice was loud and not to be interrupted. What you'd call stoned out of his skull. Shouldn't have been driving any vehicle. How he'd acquired the key to the pickup wasn't clear. Why I was with him wasn't clear. All that was clear was the high scudding moon. The high bone-glare of the moon. The two of us lurching through Highlands Park sometime beyond midnight. It was a summer-sweat night. It was a sex-sweat night. It was a night to make you want to scream, claw, tear with your teeth. I was back from college.

I was nineteen, yet. When I was nineteen, my mother had died, but that was almost a year ago, but still I was nineteen, and Roosevelt Jimson had come up to me where I'd been hanging out with some high school friends getting a buzz on at the Lakeside and I'd looked up to see him and Ohhhhhh I was hit hard. And whatever Jimson gave me to smoke, it was so sweet. That sulky-sexy mouth so sweet. Now he was pressing his foot (size of a horse-hoof, in what looked like a combat boot) against the gas pedal, then against the brake. Gas pedal. Brake. Starting up, churning gravel and stopping. Saying in his voice so loud in my ears it began to hurt, See right here. This right here. Fuck this, see! This fuckin bridge. Just wide enough for one fuckin car. It wasn't anybody Lilac knew, fuck that. Nobody who knew Lilac would've hurt her, see. It was some guy cruising the park. It was some pervert out hunting. He'd see a girl that young, looking like she's alone, and brake his car and get out and force her into the car, bullshit she'd have gotten into anybody's car by herself, Lilac was too smart for that. This guy, he'd have had to run after her maybe, drag her back to . . . Jimson's voice broke off. I couldn't look at him. I was sitting close to him in the lurching bucking pickup wanting to crawl into his lap. I was stoned out of my skull, too. Ohhhh was I stoned. Stuff I'd smoked in college was nothing like what Jimson gave me. His daddy from the Barbados, he said. His daddy's friends in Rochester. Jamming his foot against the brake pedal descending to the rattling plank bridge so that I flew forward knocking my coconut-head against the windshield. Oh Jimson! Breathless and laughing. Each time we got to the top of Ravine Road where the pickup's tires spun, throwing up gravel and stones. Each time, Jimson cursed and turned the pickup around, to descend Ravine Road another time. Headlights on bright. And there was moonlight. He'd used to come here by day, he said. For years he'd come here alone. Bring a bottle, or some stash. Sometimes he'd wake up on one of the picnic tables. He'd helped in the search for his sister. He was sixteen when she'd disappeared, a junior at the high school. He'd tramped through the woods with Mt. Olive cops and county deputies and volunteers. High-school-kid volunteers. Guys he knew, friends of his. People were mostly nice. People were wanting to help. People felt sorry for the family. People seemed to care. You wanted to find Lilac but you did not want to find Lilac's body. You wanted to find Lilac but you did not want to find Lilac in a bad way. All that tramping through the park, and police vehicles, if there'd been evidence left behind it was fucked. Maybe right away, it was fucked. And for sure it was fucked now. Ten years later. Ten years, two months. Later. His raw young furious voice, that was beginning to scare me. My sister is still missing, see. My sister, where she is, if it's just her body, what's left of her body, see, my sister was never buried right. I told my mother I would find her, I would find Lilac, if it's just her body, I would find Lilac and get her buried the right way.

Sprawled in my short red-cord skirt, flip-flops and crimson toe- and fingernails, and a kissy crimson mouth. A tank top falling off my milky shoulder. And bare beneath. I'm a pretty white-skinned girl smashed out of my skull wanting to be loved my mouth dry with the need and between my legs juiced and hurting with the need, except I am also aware of the angry young black man beside me, light-skinned gypsy-looking Lilac's big brother with some mistaken idea, Lilac was my friend, back in fifth grade Lilac liked me. And I would realize, there is danger here. If I was in a coherent frame of mind. If my hollow-coconut-head hadn't cracked against the pickup windshield that's already cracked like a cobweb. If I hadn't smoked such sweet Barbados dope. If the black man hadn't seemed to like me, I mean *me*. I mean, he'd seen me, and he'd come over to *me*. Tall and lanky and loose-jointed and with that burnt-ginger skin and big horse-eyes it didn't matter if he was good-looking or what. If he had bad intentions or what. So earnest saying, You were in Lilac's class, huh? Your father's Mr. Graf?

Wanting this wild lurching ride never to end. Thinking *Whatever happens between us.*

Vigil

"Merilee! Is that you . . ."

He'd nodded off and had now wakened abruptly. He was confused, suspicious. His ashen lips twitched in a wary smile and he fumbled to touch me as I assured him yes, I was Merilee.

". . . been here all along, Daddy. I mean, since this morning. You remember, I've been in Mt. Olive since . . . I've come to see you every day . . ."

" 'Every day'! Really."

He was heavily medicated. He was breathing through an oxygen tube attached to his nostrils. Without glasses his eyes were stark, naked, the irises dilated as if permanently shocked and the whites discolored. His face appeared drained of blood and even his hair that had been darkish gray for years seemed to have whitened. It was painful to see on his wrist a stiff paper bracelet imprinted with DENNIS W. GRAF and a lengthy computer number. He did seem happy to see me, yet uncertain why I was here. I'd explained to him several times but the effort of listening hard, trying to make sense of things, was exhausting him.

I had to lean close, to hear what he was saying. His voice was near-inaudible. All I could make out was my name *Merilee* for which I'd conceived a powerful loathing, it rang so false in the ear. Like melted candy it seemed to me. I wished that I could spit it out permanently.

I had been in Mt. Olive for four days. I had slept very little for four nights. I wasn't sure what my father remembered from one day to the next, even one hour to the next. He'd endured such a trauma, two coronary attacks within twenty-four hours. He'd been shocked back from the dead, the cardiologist explained. Probably he didn't remember that he had collapsed at home, in his study, and been brought by ambulance to Mt. Olive General Hospital; luckily, his Guatemalan housekeeper had heard him fall, and had called 911. Six days afterward he was out of intensive care and his condition was said to have "stabilized."

Relatives had warned me, your father isn't his old self.

I wasn't sure what this old self had been. I'd loved Daddy, but I hadn't ever imagined that I knew him. I'd revered him, as so many did; but I'd also feared him, distrusted and disliked him. And dreaded his judgment of me.

Oh Merilee how could you   we won't tell your father
Your father would be furious

My mother had died in this hospital. She had died of "stroke"—"seizure"—though she'd been only fifty-one. You would think, here is a mystery!—but there was no mystery. My mother, too, had been heavily medicated in the last months of her life.

I didn't want to think of Edith Graf. Not now.

My heart was filled with my father. My insides, a balloon swelling that was *Dennis Graf, my father, Daddy.* No room for anything or anyone else.

What a nightmare: he'd woken to discover plastic tubes

distending his nostrils, an IV fluid line in his battered-looking right arm, a catheter (beneath the bedclothes) jammed into his limp penis, electrodes taped to his chest and wires hooking him to a heart monitor in the nurses' station. And the demeaning little paper bracelet bearing his name and computer number.

And his daughter Merilee whom he hadn't seen in nearly two years, summoned to Mt. Olive out of an obscure and mysterious life of which he didn't approve. His daughter Merilee who was his only child, a disappointment and yet his.

Your father would be furious   we won't tell

Mornings were Daddy's best times. Sunlight flooded the tall window a few yards from the foot of his bed. It couldn't help but flatter even a sick man, how visitors wished to see Dennis Graf; how the surprisingly spacious private room was filling up with get-well cards, fresh-cut and potted flowers, baskets of fruit and gourmet foods. The nurse supervisor herself came by to check on Dennis Graf whom she recalled as "Mayor Graf." And other nurses, and orderlies. And Mt. Olive doctors who'd known him socially.

Mornings were my best time, too. Usually I fell asleep at about 3 A.M. and slept deeply until about 7 A.M. when I woke with a pounding heart and covered in sweat. The relief of morning! Thinking *If no call has come from the hospital, Daddy is still all right.*

I expected him to recover, and return home. I'd been assured by my aunt Cameron and other relatives that Daddy's heart was "mending" and if not, Dr. Lunbek advised surgery.

I brought Daddy things from home. I'd lost my key to the

house at 299 Lincoln Avenue where I'd lived the first eighteen years of my life, but my aunt had provided me with another that I might come and go at will. I brought Daddy his magazines, newspapers, a few books from his library. Though he hadn't requested it (hadn't remembered it, probably) I brought him the sculpted-glass heart.

I'd seen him use it a few times. Peering at columns of newsprint, sucking at his lips.

At other times I'd read to him. Talk to him. A bright-chattery trill like a canary's. The way nurses address patients. Especially the very sick ones, from whom you expect no reply.

"Daddy? Are you . . ."

He'd been listening to me, I thought. But by degrees his bruised eyelids drooped. His head on the concrete slab of pillow began to nod. I had been telling him about my life in New York City about which he'd always had a guarded, slightly ironic interest, as if distrusting my account of myself, guessing that I was inventing, if not frankly lying, in my effort to present a good-daughter self for his judgment. *Daddy I'm not a slut! truly* was the subtext of my appeal to the man in the cranked-up hospital bed. *Daddy don't die and leave me, I'm terrified of what will happen to me without you* for I was coming to see that I'd defined myself as Dennis Graf's daughter through my life no matter where this life was lived, or how; I'd been Dennis Graf's daughter in the way that a traveler has a home, a fixed point in space no matter how distant. *I can drift, I can stray anywhere, I am free to invent myself endlessly because there is this fixed point behind me in Mt. Olive, New York: my father Dennis Graf.*

I was dismayed, watching the old, ashen-skinned man drop into sleep. I moved the sculpted-glass heart away from the edge of his bed, where it had slipped from the newspaper page opened across his knees. I moved Daddy's blue-veined hand away from the edge of the bed where it was on the verge of slipping off. I shut my eyes, not wanting to see him. Recalling Roosevelt Jimson's face that was so alive! Livid with feeling! The deep-set horsey eyes that were heavy-lidded and down-looking as if in uncertainty then lifting suddenly to confront you, jeering. His mouth, a smile so faint it had to be jeering. I wondered if Jimson showed such a face to other blacks, individuals "of color": or just to whites?

Maybe just to white females. Maybe just to me.

I had made a fool of myself downstairs in the hospital lobby, smiling nervously at this man. Mistaken in my assumption that a smile from me would elicit, from the other, a similar friendly response. I was accustomed to such responses from both women and men. I believed that I could play both women and men in the way a practiced musician plays an instrument, if not with feeling then with a semblance of feeling. *But you have to be nice to me, I am giving you the gift of myself.*

I recalled how crazy I'd been for Roosevelt Jimson, years before. Ravine Road in the rattling pickup, and Jimson behind the wheel exuding a manic heat, and what had happened between us that night, or failed to happen.

An erotic memory to warm and excite me, in the stale-smelling air of my father's hospital room. An erotic memory to comfort me, who was beginning to feel such physical loneliness, almost I could not bear it. But Jimson wasn't the man. Jimson wasn't my man. The memory was jarring, shameful. I'd kept it at the back of my mind for more than six years. In that dark dank locked-off corner of a cellar where you hide all that you wished you could forget. I'd been reckless behaving with Lilac Jimson's older brother, I guess! Touching his bristly hair (that hadn't yet been shaved military style), his tight-muscled forearm as he gripped the steering wheel of the pickup, the tensed fist of his hand twice the size of my own. Practically crawling into the man's lap. I was nineteen, I was high on dope and beer and my own sexy self. I'd made Jimson laugh, and I'd made Jimson moan. I'd been confident that this was what I wanted, this was why I'd come with him, this was why I'd left my friends without a backward glance knowing my friends were staring after me. I'd been confident that I could handle Jimson though he wasn't anything like the boy-men with whom I'd been involved until then but somehow when Jimson began making love to me I began to be afraid of him, almost when it was too late to stop him from pushing my thighs apart and entering me I'd panicked and struggled to get away desperate to shove him off me. *No! No don't! I don't want to. I'm afraid of you.*

So ashamed! I could not bear to remember.

I must have made a sudden motion. My father, head slumped in a doze, woke suddenly, not seeming to know where he was. His eyelids fluttered, he stared at me with wild dilated eyes. "Merilee? Is that you . . ."

I told him yes. I explained I'd been in his room since that morning, I'd been here all along. It took a few seconds for this information to sink in. I wondered what the poor man saw, seeing me; the blurred figure of me seated in a chair close beside this strange cranked-up bed in a too-brightly lighted room.

Yet a crafty look came into my father's face. A signal he meant to say something funny. Maybe it would be cruel, maybe it would be cutting, but it would be funny and I should be prepared to laugh.

"Well! I've been here all along, too."

I laughed. I laughed in relief, my father's remark was funny.

Later that afternoon and evening I would repeat it for visitors, proof that my father was his own sardonic self, still.

I will be a good person, if my father is spared. I promise I will be faithful to the next man who loves me. A true gift-giver who doesn't take back the gift of herself.

He wasn't an old man: seventy-three. Not *old*.

He wanted to protest there had to be some kind of mistake.

It was true he'd had high blood pressure for years but he was taking medication wasn't he? He'd had a prostate cancer scare a few years ago but he'd caught it in time hadn't he? Yes it was true he'd had "cardiac episodes." It was true he'd had a pacemaker inserted into his chest. It was true he'd needed to lose weight, now in this shitty hospital he was losing weight wasn't he? Arms and thighs bruised from needles jabbing. His skin was turning yellow, ugly slack flabs like the skin of a plucked turkey. His vision was splotched and dazzled and his ears were like echo chambers. Couldn't sleep a normal sleep in this place, wakened through the night by needles jabbing. Wakened through the night by noises. Wakened through the night by a misery in his bowels. Maybe he'd been poisoned on one of his business trips to the Far East? Japan, China, Thailand? He hadn't been an American tourist to keep close to the Intercontinental hotels. He'd had his adventures with "natives"—he'd taken risks, been reckless. Maybe he'd picked up a rare disease, a parasite. He had a recurring nightmare, the Death Worm had burrowed through his anus, into his bowels and was threading its way into his heart. Which was why a pacemaker had been surgically inserted, to withstand the incursion of the Death Worm. He had to be free of it! He had to be free! He couldn't die yet, it was too soon!

"Merilee, help me. You have to help me. You're here to help me. I want to get the hell out of here, Merilee. Explain to the cardiologist, the son of a bitch won't listen to me. I need to be home. I can hire a nurse. Nurses. Anyone I need, I can hire. D'you know, I hired your mother? Thirty years ago. Hired your mother who was a nurse's aide, to take care of my mother. She did a good job, too. Quiet and took orders and never complained. Not like other women who think they can boss men, deceive men, not *me*. I need to get back to the house. My house. There is unfinished business in that house, I have to attend to. I have financial deals, I can't trust to anyone at the office. Your uncle Jedah is a damned smart boy but not that smart. I don't trust even him. I trust you, Merilee. The house and property are willed to you, Merilee. Jedah is the executor of the estate and you are the heiress. But I'm not ready to go, not yet. I have unfinished business. This isn't my time. I've had enough of this shit-hole, I want out. I will sue for malpractice if the sons of bitches don't let me out. I will call the chief of police, he's my friend. The district attorney, he's my friend. I'll die here, Merilee. I will die here one of these nights if I can't get out. God damn it, Merilee, help me! You're here to help me! What good are you except to help me! You've disappointed me leaving home as you did now is your chance to help your father, I want to go home today. I want to be discharged today. I can hire nurses, attendants. I can hire half the cardiac unit. I need to be home. I need to be in my home. If I am going to die, Merilee, which I don't intend to do for a long time, I want to die *at home.*"

"Your father is a seriously ill man, Miss Graf. Of course he can't 'go home.'"

In this way, days passed.

On good days, visitors came to see Dennis Graf in a steady stream. These were relatives, family friends, business acquaintances. In a special category, old political cronies. Often, eager for fresh air, I slipped away from the room at these times. I made friends with the nurses. I exclaimed at snapshots of their adorable children, I got to know their schedules. I gave them gifts for being "so nice"—"so kind"—to my difficult father. I struck up an edgy bantering acquaintance with a night-attendant named André. He was hulking-tall, with a pasty pitted skin and jutting jaw, brooding shy-boy Hispanic eyes. I calculated his age as approximately my own, maybe a little older. A wedding band glinted on his left hand. We laughed together, with a sound like startled shore-birds. I embarrassed him by insisting that he take some of the useless gourmet gifts that were accumulating in my father's room—chocolate-covered truffles, fruit-flavored liqueurs, candied apricots, pistachios and Brazil nuts. Afterward I would see André gazing covertly at me along the length of the corridor as if trying to figure me out.

I want to make love with you but I guess it won't happen.

I want my father to recover and come home but I guess it won't happen.

Please André can you help me! I'm not sure how.

Once, I sighted a tall light-skinned black man in the parking garage adjacent to the hospital. He was walking away from me. I couldn't see his face, he wore a baseball cap with the rim pulled low. He wore tan trousers, a lime-green sport shirt. He moved briskly with the ease of an ex-athlete. Maybe he'd sighted me, maybe not. It had been an exhausting and depressing day at the hospital and I wasn't feeling very vivid, or even visible—as if, if you'd glance at me, you might not see anyone here. I'd been out of my father's room two or three times that day and so Jimson might have dropped by to visit my father without my knowing. Nor would my father have mentioned him since, when visitors left his room and were replaced by others, he tended to forget them all.

I followed after the light-skinned black man at a distance, not certain if he was Jimson who'd stepped out of the elevator in the hospital lobby to confront me, or a stranger. I was breathing, anxious. Wanting to run after him pleading *Let me try again! This time will be different.*

"Jesus! This one thing I'm learning."

My father meant to speak vehemently but his words sounded like dry reeds stirred in a hot dry wind.

He seemed distressed. He'd been trying to read, using the sculpted-glass heart, but his glasses kept sliding down his nose as if they'd become too large for his thinning face. I reached out to touch the blue-veined back of his hand.

"Daddy, what? What are you learning?"

He tried to speak, but his mouth was too dry. I handed him a glass of water, and helped him drink. Frustrated and confused he repeated what sounded like, ". . . one thing I'm learning, this . . . *this is it.*"

Another time he said, rubbing the heel of his hand against his sunken chest, "They'd run me for mayor again, they said. Soon as I get out of this place. Those bastards, d'you think they mean it?"

I pushed my father in a wheelchair around the Cardiology Unit block. Twice around, at a dignified pace.

Greeting the nurses. Mostly young, buoyant, pretty nurses with canary-trill voices like my own.

"Mr. Graf! Good morning."

"Mr. Graf, Merilee—real nice day today, in'it?"

You couldn't see much of the sunny late-June day but it did appear to be one of Daddy's good mornings. It was an opportunity for me to say, as if I'd just now thought of it, "Daddy? When you first met Mom . . ." But the words faded even as I spoke. *Nurse's aide. Quiet and took orders and never complained.* While she'd been alive I had been embarrassed and annoyed and impatient with my mother, did I deserve hearing about her now? I did not.

Daddy's room was empty! Daddy's hospital bed. He'd been taken away on a gurney, IV fluids attached, for another defibrillation ordeal. His faulty heart stopped, and forcibly restarted. It was a procedure requiring electricity, little bolts of lightning as in a lurid Frankenstein movie you'd see on late-night TV.

Aunt Cameron and I remained behind in the room. Just when I'd been getting to know my aunt, Daddy's older sister, who'd always intimidated me with her brisk brusque stylish manner, as she'd intimidated my mother, this pale-blond-haired woman of seventy-five was beginning to show her age. Talking in a hurt, befuddled voice of "what will they do to Dennis next" as if Daddy's medical misfortunes were the fault of his physicians. And she couldn't comprehend why her younger brother, only seventy-three, wasn't a good risk for a heart transplant.

I held my aunt's chill limp hand, to comfort her. Even the bones of her hand felt contentious.

Needing comfort myself! For I could not imagine in which direction my life would swerve, if my father died.

I'd left New York City abruptly. When my aunt called to summon me home, I had come immediately. I'd used the opportunity to resign from a job that bored me, and to break up with a man who'd begun to bore me. The job had been assistant to the executive director of an arts foundation that gave away millions of dollars in fellowship grants each year, and the man, in his fifties, a quite nice man, had been the executive director of the foundation. He had called me numerous times on my cell phone since I'd left New York but I hadn't been able to force myself to return his calls just yet. *What am I doing here in Mt. Olive, I am keeping vigil. I am waiting.*

In New York, I'd led a slapdash sort of life. It had not been a serious life perhaps. I lived in borrowed apartments, or with friends like my married-man-friend the foundation director. I hadn't much money of my own but I rarely lacked for money. I wore stylish clothes, shoes. Frequently there'd been mornings when, waking in a place not immediately known to me, I'd invented a Merilee appropriate to the occasion, with much success.

Often I was complimented: how pretty you are! how happy you make others, by your presence!

Thinking *Yes but only pretty. Not beautiful.*

Yes but the happiness is only for others, not me. And don't imagine you can rely upon it.

My New York life was rapidly fading like a dream, vivid and enthralling while it lasts, that begins to disappear as soon as you open your eyes. You feel a pang of loss, maybe a flurry of panic at what you are losing, then it's gone.

Daddy had called me his "heiress"—"my heiress." *Heiress* was so formal-sounding, it filled me with dread. I understood that my father was a rich man, at least by Mt. Olive standards, he would leave behind a considerable estate. Even if much of it was willed to local charities, as expected, Daddy's principal heiress would probably receive several million dollars, at the least. And there was the old cobblestone house on Lincoln Avenue, given "landmark" status and a gleaming brass plaque by the New York State Historical Society, of which Daddy had been so proud: I could not imagine inheriting that house! I had only vague vaporish memories of having lived in it for eighteen years. Back in Mt. Olive I was staying at the home of a girl cousin, not at the old house, though I'd been unclear about this, when Daddy had asked me if I was back in my "old room."

Thinking *The dying are easy to lie to!*

Then, immediately repentant, thinking *I will make it up to Daddy, I will live in that house.*

My mother, too, had "collapsed" in the house. In an upstairs bathroom, apparently in the middle of the night; her body wasn't found by my father until morning. After she was buried I hadn't been able to force myself to remain in Mt. Olive long enough to sort through her things, leaving the task to my capable aunt Cameron and other female relatives, and most of her few possessions had been given to Goodwill or discarded. I'd told my aunt that I hadn't wanted anything of my mother's, thank you. If there were photographs of my mother as a younger woman, these too seemed to have been lost. Or someone (maybe my mother herself, in one of her nerved-up moods) had destroyed them.

Impulsively I said, "Aunt Cameron? Did you know my mother

when Daddy first met her? You must have—she'd been a nurse's aide for your mother?"

Aunt Cameron looked sharply at me, as if like a brash ignorant child I'd inadvertently uttered something obscene.

"Who on earth told you that, Merilee? Who's been saying such things?"

Aunt Cameron tugged her hand out of mine. Her attractive, softly lined face, immaculately made up each morning in a subtly scented pale-peach powder, flushed with annoyance.

"Daddy told me. The other day. He was upset and he began telling me about a number of things, he'd mentioned that Mom had been—"

"I don't care to discuss your mother's background, Merilee. Edith was an unhappy woman, though your father gave her everything she could ask for. May she rest in peace."

"But, Aunt Cameron—"

My aunt heaved herself to her feet, fierce and indignant. She stood no more than five feet one but exuded the authoritative air of one much larger. I saw her glancing toward the doorway as if she feared someone drifting by and overhearing us, or, worse yet, visitors stepping into the room.

Yet I persisted: "Mom never seemed to want anything, did she? At least not—"

Aunt Cameron dealt with my obstinance by leaving the room. Her parting words were delivered with theatrical economy and aplomb:

"*May she rest in peace.* That's quite enough on the subject."

•   •   •

There'd been a feeling of dread. A feeling of not-wanting-to-go-home. Cautiously climbing the back stairs where the silly old snakes slept in the worn carpet, no longer feared. And passing by my mother's bathroom where the door, oh the damned door!—wasn't this just like my mother—was partly open and inside my mother was coughing, or choking, or vomiting in the most repulsive way, I could not bear to hear. I was twelve or thirteen, still in middle school. My girlfriends were waiting for me a few blocks away at another girl's house. Maybe I hesitated hearing my mother in distress but no, no!—I wasn't going to knock on the door to see what was wrong, I didn't want to know what was wrong.

Didn't then, and didn't now.

Keeping a hospital vigil, you begin to wear out your smile-face.

Soon you've given gifts to everyone on the staff. Soon you're known to everyone on the staff. Soon, some of the staff begin to avoid you out of pity if not impatience.

Downstairs in the coffee shop where I'd befriended some of the staff and struck up conversations with interns, nurses, orderlies, one evening the TV was turned to CNN breaking news in Oxnard, California, where a search team was looking for a missing nine-year-old girl believed to have been abducted by an unknown person or persons from a playground. There were aerial views of police officers and volunteers trudging through an area of dry grasses and scrub trees. There were loud men with bullhorns, roadblocks and low-flying helicopters.

Talk in the coffee shop shifted to other missing girls. Lilac Jimson was named.

"... that poor little colored girl, wasn't it? Just disappeared without a trace that'd been how long ago ..."

"Well, they say ..."

"Say what?"

"... people know what happened to her. Some people. That's what we heard."

"... some kind of revenge, for her father mixed up with drug dealers he owed money to? That's what I heard."

"*I* heard, the girl ran off. Had a fight with her mother, and ran away with some man down to Jamaica."

" 'Some man'? The girl was only eleven."

"Well—eleven. Some kinds of ethnic cultures, girls grow up fast."

I'd been listening to these remarks intending to remain silent but now I was upset. Setting down my coffee cup, pushing my chair back from the table. Hot fists of blood pounded in my face and I couldn't trust myself to speak. I saw startled eyes on me, and hurried out of the coffee shop.

I knew Lilac! Lilac was my friend. She didn't run away she was taken. No one has ever found her not even her bones.

A morning in early July. Daddy's nineteenth day at Mt. Olive General Hospital.

When I arrived at room four-fourteen, he wasn't there. His bed was empty. I felt a moment's vertigo thinking *Has he died? Have they taken him away? Wouldn't they have informed me?* My heart pounded with anxiety and almost a kind of hope, that the ordeal of waiting would be ended, so abruptly, but in fact my father had been taken away to Radiology for an MRI exam and a husky male attendant, not André, was deftly stripping off soiled and smelly bedclothes to replace them with new. How striking a physical presence the attendant was, coppery flesh rippling at the back of his neck. He was stocky, with thick upper arms and thighs. He was whistling under his breath taking pleasure in a task he performed with mechanical precision: unmaking a bed, re-making a bed. Fascinated I watched his expert hands and imagined them on me. Caressing or squeezing, pummeling, slapping—such hands would act of their own volition, not mine.

The attendant glanced around and saw me then. His whistle faded. He mumbled what sounded like "H'lo ma'am" and quickly finished with the bed.

"Daddy? See."

I was wearing the pink-pearl necklace from long ago. I'd brought it with me to Mt. Olive thinking that my father would be pleased to see it around my neck after so many years.

Daddy peered up at me over his glasses. He'd been squinting at the front page of the Rochester newspaper. With painstaking slowness moving the sculpted-glass heart down columns of newsprint.

"The pearl necklace you gave me, remember? It was for my birthday, I was just a little girl. It belonged to . . ."

Daddy's lips twitched in a mildly perplexed smile. He was breathing raspily through the oxygen tubes. There seemed to be comprehension in his watery eyes as I tried to explain, the necklace was a "family heirloom" that had once belonged to his mother, my grandmother Graf who'd died when I was a little girl. "It's the most beautiful, precious thing I own, Daddy. Which I never wear except on special occasions."

Maybe this was true. Maybe it was bullshit. Daddy frowned as if deliberating. It wasn't clear whether he remembered the necklace Mom had so fussed over. "But what is the 'special occasion' now, Merilee?" Daddy's left eyelid drooped in a sly wink.

Helen was the senior cardiology nurse. Most admired, most feared by the younger nurses. Helen was in her fifties, squat-bodied with a solid bulldog face and brass-colored hair. I had overheard her scolding a young nurse named Donna, one of the nurses assigned to my father. I had befriended Helen with gifts of Godiva chocolates and a vase of flowers when gifts to Daddy threatened to overwhelm his room. One day I paid Helen's bill in the coffee shop below: coffee, Danish pastry. I'd been asking Helen about her background, her training. I'd been asking Helen about her life as a nurse so that I could ask her what I'd planned to ask from the first: if she'd met or known a young nurse's aide named Edith Schechter in the 1970s, in Mt. Olive, and Helen asked me to repeat the name, and frowned thoughtfully, wiping crumbs from her mouth, as if trying sincerely to recall, but could not. "Who was 'Edith Schechter'?" Helen asked me and I said, "I don't know. I was hoping you could tell me."

• • •

In the cardiologist's office I began to cry. Dr. Lunbek shielded a direct view of me with a hand nervously stroking his comb-over beige hair.

The decision was: Dennis Graf wasn't strong enough for heart valve surgery.

This was a relief! But no, this was not a relief for his strained heart was gradually "failing."

In the hard-backed chair in which I was sitting, an adult daughter of a doomed father, I cried mostly soundlessly, but also pointlessly. This was still the day of the pink-pearl necklace. This was still the day of the special occasion. This was the effort of a pretty-though-ravaged-looking girl in a white linen blouse with demure boxy sleeves in a retro style, suggesting the 1940s. My tailored beige linen trousers fitted me now loosely for I'd lost weight since returning to Mt. Olive but the trousers were spotless and neatly creased, I had risen early to iron them that morning in my cousin's house. As my father's health was deteriorating and I was becoming exhausted, like a juicy melon whose insides are being scraped dry, still I made myself up carefully each morning, never failed to wash and blow-dry my shiny dark hair, and wore my few changes of high-quality clothes meant to draw glances of admiration from both women and men.

I had sexier, more eye-catching clothes, I did not intend to wear in Mt. Olive.

Dr. Lunbek had been speaking. I'd seen his mouth move. He had explained my father's physical condition in more detail than I would have liked to hear yet still I seemed to be pleading with him with my tearful eyes until he said, frowning, as if the words were being shaken out of him, "But maybe, later . . ."

I reached for Dr. Lunbek's hands, snaring just one. My face streamed tears. I knew, despite my heirloom pearls, ladylike clothes and makeup I looked like hell. I heard myself stammering thank you, thank you Dr. Lunbek: "Anything you can do for my father, I will be so . . ."

Lunbek stared at me in alarm and embarrassment. If initially he'd been attracted by my pretty face and clothes, he wasn't so attracted now, though he was gracious enough to let me knead his hand like a frightened child. Quickly he rose to his feet but took care to remain behind his desk, and to keep the desk between us.

This strange thing. I remember.

Detaching the sculpted-glass heart from my father's slack fingers when he'd drifted off to sleep. Holding the glass against the newspaper page he'd been reading and here was a column of newsprint like agitated ants, and here was a luridly colored photograph of fallen and disfigured bodies amid rubble, somewhere in Iraq where our powerful and vindictive country was at war.

Magnified, the bodies expanded to myriad gray dots and quickly lost definition. I remembered my father saying, years ago, "If you look too closely at people, we are all alike—material. And if you look yet more closely, we are all atoms in the void—energy."

I'd shivered at the thought. And shivered now bringing the sculpted-glass heart against the back of my father's hand where the veins were swollen and the skin was discolored and creases nearly invisible to the naked eye became rivulets.

Daddy's eyelids fluttered but did not open. Where he drifted now, I could not follow and could not imagine. *Why didn't you love me, Daddy* is not a question an adult daughter can reasonably ask of her dying father as *Why don't you like me, Lilac* not a question a ten-year-old girl could ask of a classmate.

I brought the glass heart up close against my father's slack, sallow face, his drooping mouth, the wet glisten of dentures unnaturally white like laundry detergent. I was fascinated even as I was repelled seeing stubble like metal filings pushing through the skin—for what purpose was a beard on the face of an elderly man?

Almost, I could hear my father's rasping voice. "One thing I'm learning, *this is it.*"

When I drew the glass heart away from the surface of my father's skin, the magnification increased until finally a single crease, a single whorl, a single liver spot, expanded to fit the entire heart. As I continued to lift the heart toward my eye, everything became blurred, blind.

Visitors to see my father had mostly stopped coming by the end of June.

And now, Daddy didn't care to see anyone except his closest relatives, and not always them.

For weeks there'd been a steady procession of well-wishers. Half of Mt. Olive must have made the pilgrimage to see Dennis Graf in his hospital bed. Old friends, distant relatives, neighbors and business associates and fellow members of the First Presbyterian Church of Mt. Olive, fellow Chautauqua County republicans nostalgic about the "wild times" in the 1980s when Dennis Graf had been a popular mayor of Mt. Olive for two four-year terms.

Several recipients of Graf Scholarships to the local community college and tech school, the police academy and the nursing school at Rochester, came by to thank Daddy. They appeared to be strangers to him, uncomfortable and nervous in the presence of the elderly man.

One of them was Roosevelt Jimson.

"Daddy? A visitor for you . . ."

He'd knocked diffidently on the part-opened door. Seeing me he'd mumbled a vague greeting. He had not come to speak with me but with my father, that was clear.

It was late in Daddy's illness. I wondered why Jimson had postponed seeing him. Awkward as he was, staring at Daddy in his cranked-up hospital bed, Jimson was visibly ill at ease like one to whom the sight of a very sick man was alarming.

Daddy was watching, or anyway gazing at, the (muted) TV positioned above his bed, tuned to CNN. His watery eyes slid onto Jimson as if grudgingly. Maybe he recognized Jimson, maybe not. Jimson mumbled, "H'lo, Mr. Graf. Heard you weren't feeling too well . . ." He was wearing a navy blue T-shirt tucked into work trousers and carried the grimy baseball cap in his hand. I saw how the arrogant younger man effaced himself before the elder man and didn't know how I felt about this. Jimson's natural self was surly, mocking. You just knew how in his heart he scorned whites, at least whites of privilege like my father, and me. Yet his demeanor at Daddy's bedside seemed genuine. He didn't seem to loom so tall and even his bristling goatee seemed subdued.

From Jimson's murmured remarks I understood that he'd gone to the Rochester Police Academy on a Graf Scholarship, he'd graduated two years before and had been a rookie officer on the Mt. Olive force until recently. If I'd been involved in the conversation I might have asked Jimson what had happened, wasn't he a police officer any longer, but I'd quietly removed myself to a rear corner of the room to make calls on my cell phone, to relatives who'd been leaving messages on my father's answering service. If Jimson glanced in my direction, I wasn't looking in his.

When, after a few awkward minutes Jimson mumbled goodbye to my father and left the room, cap in hand, I remained where I was and didn't follow after him. Thinking *The hell with you. I don't need your black prick, or you.*

I stood by my father's bedside. Again his eyes had lifted to the (muted) TV screen. Though newspapers, magazines, paperback books had accumulated on his bedside table, Daddy rarely tried to read any longer. He was breathing through the oxygen tube with an audible hiss. I asked him if he knew who his visitor was, the man who'd just been here to see him, and Daddy's slack lips twitched in a vague smile, or maybe it was a grimace, for obviously he hadn't known, and hadn't much interest in being told.

"You probably didn't hear his name, he didn't speak very clearly—'Roosevelt Jimson.' The older brother of Lilac. You remember, the lost girl."

I'd never spoken of Lilac as "lost" before. It was a gentler way of saying *taken.*

My father's eyes shifted from the TV screen, rapidly he began to blink. He stared into a corner of the room as I spoke to him and though muscles in his jaws tightened, he did not speak.

". . . he was saying how grateful he was, Daddy, that you

helped him with his education. And you'd helped his mother, financially. After his sister was . . . After Lilac disappeared."

He'd helped in the search, too. In Highlands Park, in the deep treacherous ravine that ran twisting and meandering through Mt. Olive and into the countryside. He'd tramped with other searchers along the banks of the Chautauqua River and into the foothills of the Chautauqua Mountains. It was an open secret that he'd pledged most of the $20,000 reward money. It had been frustrating, and it had infuritated him, that Lilac Jimson had never been found, yet the tragedy had happened long ago now, he seemed only vaguely to remember.

A forlorn old man in a hospital bed, attached to IV fluids, an oxygen tank, and beneath the bedclothes a catheter. His parched lips moved in a whisper, ". . . 'Jimson.' That little gypsy-girl . . ."

"Alina's daughter, Daddy, remember? She was eleven when it happened. She was in my fifth-grade class at the Thomas Jefferson school. 'Lilac Jimson,' her name and picture were on all those posters, back in 1988, everyone searched for her but she was never found."

Daddy was staring into a corner of the room. His reddened eyelids blinked in the effort of remembering. With the heel of his right hand he rubbed his sunken chest, in the area of his heart. He'd hated the pacemaker inserted into the muscles encasing the heart, in one of his angry despairing moods he'd threatened to tear it out.

I leaned over my father, to hear what he was trying to say. My nostrils constricted smelling the slightly acrid odor of his bedridden body. The rank odor of my own animal panic, I'd managed to disguise with a flowery-sweet cologne. ". . . never found? Never? *Never found?*" Daddy's eyes opened wide, showing a rim of white above the iris. I tried to calm him, taking hold of his hands, but he threw me off, agitated.

"Don't touch! Who are . . . *you!*"

It was the final hour of my vigil.

Next morning at 5:20 A.M., Dennis Graf would be pronounced dead of heart failure. The death-call, to his daughter Merilee, would come soon after.

Missing

Now we saw her everywhere.

Lilac Jimson had disappeared and yet: Lilac's face was everywhere we looked.

On TV. In newspapers. On walls, fences, telephone poles. On tree trunks. Posters blossoming like exotic yellow flowers with tall urgent black letters.

MISSING 11-YR-OLD
LILAC JIMSON
4'8"   73 lbs
brown eyes/black hair
white T-shirt/green shorts
red hair ribbons
last seen May 14 Highlands Park

IF YOU HAVE INFORMATION
CALL MT. OLIVE POLICE
(716) 373-8245
$20,000 REWARD

It was scary to see Lilac's smiling face in a picture snipped out of a family photograph. Smiling so hard, like nothing was wrong. Lilac's sparkly eyes, Lilac's pierced ears, the wink of the gold filling between two front teeth, the tight-braided hair springing out from her head tied with two red ribbons. I was fearful of looking too closely into Lilac's eyes for what if Lilac could look into my eyes in return? What you were made to realize staring at Lilac's smiling face was that when the picture was taken Lilac hadn't any idea what would happen to her. *I am just like you* Lilac seemed to be saying. *What happened to me can happen to you.*

I shut my eyes. I tried not to see. I tried not to cry. I ran to hide. I hid in my room. I hid in my bed. I pulled the covers over my head but still I saw Lilac's face. I saw her eyes fixed on me. I saw the great eagle swoop down to seize her by the shoulders and carry her away screaming into the sky and I felt the talons in my shoulders and screamed but no sound came from my throat dry as sand.

"They won't ever find her, will they? Is Lilac dead?"

Dead was a new word for me. A new daring word for me to speak aloud. At school it was whispered, you would not want any teacher to overhear.

Lilac is dead that's what happened to her. Why she isn't in school anymore.

My mother pretended not to hear my question. If I asked her a wrong question sometimes she would not seem to hear but sometimes she became upset. Angry tears sprang into her eyes and her hands clenched into fists but she never touched me. Since Lilac had been taken two weeks ago I said things I didn't really mean, silly things a little girl might ask not a ten-year-old in fifth grade. "If Lilac is dead will they bury her in the cemetery? In the *ground?*"

I laughed, it was so icky. In the ground!

Still my mother, parking her car in the lot behind Rexall's Drugs, seemed not to hear. Since picking me up from school she'd been distracted, edgy. Biting at her raw-looking lower lip and muttering to herself. The parking lot was cramped and crowded and Mom was having a difficult time backing into a space. Her car was big and boxy and shiny-black. Mom was anxious about scraping a fender. The more anxious Mom was, the more likely it would happen (for it had happened with previous cars in similar circumstances) that she would scrape or dent a fender. In reverse the heavy car bucked and lurched. In reverse Mom craned her neck to peer into the rearview mirror with a look of pain. Tears shimmered in her eyes but did not spill over. The lipstick she'd smeared on her mouth before leaving home was greasy-red and vivid as neon in her chalky-white face. Her dust-colored hair was stiff and unwashed beneath a kerchief tied at her chin. I was embarrassed of my mother for no one else's mother wore a dowdy kerchief tied tight beneath her chin on even cold winter days, and this was a spring day so warm and bright it hurt your eyes.

There was a hurt in my throat, too. My voice rose recklessly to make my mother hear: "Is she? *Is* she? *Is Lilac dead?*"

Mom braked the car, abruptly. She'd given up trying to maneuver into the parking space and would leave the car at a crooked angle, blocking the way of other drivers if they wanted to exit the lot. She was in a hurry to get into the drugstore before it closed, she said. Had to get her prescription filled.

Mom was breathless telling me that she would lock the car so that nobody could "get" me here while she was gone.

I asked if I could come with her but Mom ignored me. I watched her walk quickly to the rear entrance of Rexall's, almost running in her stumpy-heeled brown leather shoes.

I was only ten but I seemed to know: the drugstore wasn't anywhere near closing at 3:30 P.M. of a weekday.

I had come to hate how, because of Lilac, my mother would not allow me to walk home from school any longer. Every morning she insisted upon driving me and every afternoon she insisted upon picking me up arriving early before the bell rang so that I had to run out to the big boxy shiny-black car parked at the curb when I wanted to stay behind with my friends. It was only three blocks from Thomas Jefferson Elementary to Lincoln Avenue at the top of a long hill, and one more block to our house, but my mother refused to allow me to walk even with other, older children for what if I was taken away? What if I was kidnapped? "You know who would be blamed," my mother said with a hurt little laugh. "—Me."

This was meant to be funny, I think. Or maybe, the way Mom sighed and picked at her face as if she wanted to draw blood, it wasn't.

Often lately, when Mom picked me up from school, she had to "drop by" a drugstore. There were two drugstores in downtown Mt. Olive and another drugstore at the Northland Mall which was a mile outside town and Mom had prescriptions with each. There were different doctors for different drugs for each store, maybe. Often I overheard Mom speaking sharply on the phone with doctors and pharmacists. It was a serious matter, if Mom ran out of a prescription drug. If Mom was "running low." I understood that certain of my mother's drugs were more important than others. There were drugs for "nerves" and drugs for "stomach" and drugs for "headache" and drugs for "sleep" and drugs for "tension" and drugs for "pain." Occasionally there were special temporary drugs, like antibiotics, for short-term illnesses. Some of these drugs were small round white pills and some were chalky oblong pills so large they had to be cut carefully in two by Mom, with a knife blade. But Mom's most precious drugs were small capsules that were half dark-green and half light-green and felt like plastic. I asked what the capsules were for and Mom smiled mysteriously and said that was a secret, I was too young to be told. I asked how you could swallow something made of plastic and Mom said don't be silly, the capsules were not plastic but some material that would melt in your stomach. Talking of her favorite drugs, Mom seemed almost happy. I saw that her eyes were a shimmery gray-green almost the shade of the lighter green half of the capsules. I asked if I could have a capsule and Mom quickly said no. I asked why not and Mom said because. I asked why "because" and Mom said because I was too young. But Mom was staring at me. Like she was seeing someone else, in me. Suddenly changing her mind saying, All right I could have just half a capsule because I was half her size.

Carefully Mom cut a capsule in two with a knife—"Half for you, Merilee, and half for me." Mom brought a glass of cold milk for me, and a glass of dark wine for herself. We swallowed the capsule halves sitting together on a rattan sofa in the sunroom of the big dark cobblestone house where most rooms had leaded-glass windows that provided little light. A few yards away on a marble-topped table was a foot-high sandstone statue Daddy had brought back from one of his travels to what he called the Far East. The statue was a fattish man seated with his legs and bare feet twisted strangely beneath him. His face was broad and expressionless, his eyes were empty and unjudging. "That stone man with the blind eyes is a god," my mother said. "Millions of people worship him because he's a blind god." It was strange for my mother to speak to me in such a way as she might have spoken to another adult (though I rarely heard her speak to any adult including even my father) and so I felt privileged but had no idea how to reply. "He is 'Buddha' and he teaches the path to 'Nirvana' which is the cessation of all desire. Your father brought that back from Thailand when you were a baby." I finished my glass of milk that was so chalky-cold it made my forehead ache. Mom finished her glass of dark wine and poured herself another. I began to feel sleepy, dreamy. I told Mom about a book I was reading, one of the Black Stallion books which were my favorites, and Mom was stroking the back of my hand as if to encourage me to speak which wasn't like her. And suddenly my tongue began to feel thick. And my head was heavy. And my eyelids were heavy. There was a quivering shadow on the floor at our feet, I leaned over to see what it was and suddenly I fell into it, and was gone.

When I opened my eyes, I was lying stiffly on the rattan sofa, beneath a wool blanket. It was dark. Dark in the sunroom, and dark outside.

Our secret, Merilee! Never to be repeated and never to be told to anyone especially not your father.

• • •

As soon as my mother slid behind the wheel of the car she tore the white drugstore package open. Her shaky fingers managed to unscrew the vial top, shook two shiny green capsules onto the palm of her hand and swallowed them down, dry.

"Thank God."

This breathy exclamation wasn't meant for me to hear.

The capsules were magic drugs, I knew. I was fearful of them remembering how sleepy I'd become, how tired, how long I had slept and my stiff neck, parched throat and aching watering eyes afterward, still I understood that they were magic if you were an adult and if you were Edith Graf for already within minutes Mom was calmer. She'd ceased gnawing at her lower lip. She drove the big boxy car without nearly so much effort as before, maintaining a slow, steady speed through the business section of Mt. Olive and so to South Main, and Second Street, and eventually, on higher ground, the big cobblestone house at 299 Lincoln Avenue that was surrounded by a five-foot black wrought-iron fence, tall trees and ornamental shrubs. By the time we pulled into the driveway my mother had ceased breathing quickly and her eyes glancing over me were empty and unjudging as the eyes of the blind Buddha from Thailand.

"By now, the bastard is probably a thousand miles away. And the little girl . . ."

I'd never heard my father speak in such a tone of weary disgust.

I'd never heard my father speak so openly, loudly on the telephone in his study, having forgotten to shut the door.

Daddy had taken time off from his office at Graf Imports, Inc. to help with the search for Lilac though he wasn't, as he had to concede, a young man any longer. He'd taken for granted that he was in good condition, he'd been maybe a little vain of his physical strength and stamina, yet it was damned hard to keep up with the others hiking through woods, in the Highlands ravine and trudging through underbrush and marshland along the Chautauqua River. One of his friends he'd known since high school was a search volunteer alongside his twenty-two-year-old firefighter son and this man, fifty-seven, Daddy's exact age, had had an angina attack the previous day, had to be taken by ambulance to the hospital. It was just that Daddy was so angry! Damned mad! He'd known the little girl, he'd once hired her mother as a cleaning woman. He'd put pressure on the New York State police to help in the investigation, and if they'd acted faster, if the FBI had become involved, if "damned amateur" police departments in other jurisdictions had been more cooperative, by now Lilac Jimson might be back with her family and the sick bastard who'd taken her behind bars.

Seeing me outside his study door, Daddy grimaced, gestured for me to go away, and came to shut the door.

Except for telling me never to talk with strangers, to report any stranger who approached me or my friends or who loitered in the vicinity of my school, my father did not speak with me about my missing classmate. He instructed my mother not to allow me to watch television news or see the newspapers but it was easy for me to get hold of newspapers after they'd been stacked for the trash in a corner of the kitchen. As I was frightened and fascinated by the yellow-bordered MISSING posters so I was frightened and fascinated by newspaper headlines. The name JIMSON leapt at me out of a swirl of newsprint. LILAC JIMSON. MISSING FIFTH GRADER. Such headlines as SEARCH CONTINUES FOR MISSING MT. OLIVE GIRL. CHAUTAUQUA CO. POLICE "BAFFLED" IN MISSING-CHILD CASE. FEW LEADS IN SEARCH FOR 11-YEAR-OLD. HIGHLANDS PARK ABDUCTION CASE IN FOURTH WEEK, NO RANSOM DEMANDS. There had been numerous calls to authorities by well-intentioned individuals but no helpful information was said to have been received by police. There were no candidates for the $20,000 reward. Newspapers reported witnesses claiming to have seen vehicles with out-of-state license plates cruising Highlands Park in the area of the picnic grove from which it was believed Lilac had disappeared, a sighting of "strangers" in the park. A "dark-skinned"—"foreign-looking"— man, or men. A man with a mustache, wearing dark glasses. A man wearing dapper "city-type" clothes. A man wearing work clothes "like a janitor." A man in his thirties. Middle-aged. Tall, above six feet. Short and heavyset "like a fire hydrant."

Lilac's father had been interrogated, exhaustively. For a few days he'd been in "protective custody" at Mt. Olive Police headquarters. It was generally believed that Raoul Jimson knew more than he was willing to confess, for Jimson had a criminal record (narcotics, suspected burglaries in Port Oriskany) and was at this time on county probation for passing forged checks. It was believed that others in the Jimson family including Lilac's mother Alina, her older sisters and sixteen-year-old brother Roosevelt, a sophomore at Mt. Olive High with a history of being a "troublemaker," knew more than they were willing to confess but nothing could be proven, police had had to let all the Jimsons go.

Avidly I read everything I could lay my hands on. I had always been an eager reader and now at age ten, I became an insatiable reader of newspapers, some of them taken from the trash cans of our neighbors. Except it was only news of Lilac Jimson that excited me. That leap in my heart at the sighting of JIMSON amid newsprint.

It was claimed that, before Lilac, no child so young had ever disappeared in Chautauqua County, which was mostly rural and uncultivated. Older girls and boys had run away from home and numerous adults had vanished of their own volition or otherwise but no child of eleven had been taken in such a way, not ever. I thought that Lilac would be proud, if she'd known. In school she'd always basked in attention, especially in gym class where she'd been so monkey-nimble and fast leaving most of the other girls behind. (I was a fast runner, too. And I was pretty good on the rings and ropes. But nothing like Lilac who our gym teacher said was a "natural.")

No one so young had been taken from Chautauqua County but in Port Oriskany, which was forty miles to the west, on Lake Erie, two girls, nine and fourteen, had disappeared and never been found within the past several years; and in Chautauqua Falls, eighteen miles to the east, a fourteen-year-old girl had vanished in May 1987. In the *Mt. Olive Journal,* photographs of these missing girls were printed with the photograph of Lilac Jimson and it was a shock to see how the missing girls resembled one another, like sisters.

Aunt Cameron was relieved: "See, Edith! There's no danger to our Merilee, these are all little colored girls."

The Littlest Doll

W hen the call came. At 5:45 A.M. Yanking me from the sweet black muck of sleep still as death. Informing me *Miss Graf? Your father has passed away.* And I'd been so still, in sleep. And I'd been dreaming a silent slow-motion dream. Seeming to know (in the dream, as perhaps I hadn't altogether known in life) that my father hadn't loved me, I had never been the daughter he'd wished for. As my mother had not been the wife he'd wished for. This was my secret, I must live with. In my dream I smiled, my mouth twisted in the effort of smiling, to think, yes I can handle such a secret. For I was the kind of girl (though twenty-six, more girl than woman) in which such secrets might be hidden. Like those charming/unnerving Tibetan dolls-within-dolls my father used to import. These were carved female figures in colorful peasant costumes. You gripped the doll firmly in two hands and tugged at it, the upper half came away from the lower half, and inside was a second, smaller female figure in a similar peasant costume; you opened this figure, and inside was a third, smaller figure; you continued until you came upon the smallest figure, the littlest doll, about the size of your little finger, a girl-child with glossy painted-on black hair and sparkly black eyes.

I thought, I can do this. I was the littlest doll, but also the others. But no one would tug me apart.

Gone

The sculpted-glass heart!

It wasn't on the bedside table where I'd seen it last (how many days ago?) and it wasn't inside the drawer (with Daddy's wristwatch) and it wasn't on the shelf below with a pile of news-papers and magazines. I squatted to look on the floor beneath the table, a tangle of electrical outlets. On hands and knees I looked beneath the stripped-bare bed. I was cursing, whimper-ing like a kicked dog. "Oh damn. Oh shit. Fuck. It can't be! Can't be gone." Where for weeks there'd been a gallon-sized plastic container for Daddy's urine beneath the bed, now there was nothing.

Blood rushed into my head. Arteries in my brain close to bursting.

I scrambled to my feet. I checked the drawer again. The top of the bureau, the drawers of the bureau. I pawed through things on the windowsill—get-well cards, flowers in clay pots wrapped in tinsel, wicker baskets of gourmet foods. I heard my breath, quickened and panting.

I couldn't let myself think the sculpted-glass heart had been stolen. For then it might be gone forever.

Desperate, I even looked in the small bathroom that opened

off my father's room. I was half-sobbing, pathetic. Peering into the shower stall. As if the glass heart could be in the shower stall. I was feeling faint, so hit by alarm, fury. I had to pause, to recover my breath. Wiping at my eyes. Daddy had died only a few hours before, and now the sculpted-glass heart was gone. But it couldn't be gone.

In the shower there was a wooden stool. I was struck by a sudden vision of an elderly infirm person, naked, with a sallow sunken chest and distended potbelly, seated on this stool as an attendant ran the shower and bathed him, as you might bathe a very young child; I saw the man's meekly bowed head, thin gray hair in wet strands against the egg-dome of his head. The vision came to me raw and powerful as a hallucination.

I backed away. I fled into the outer room.

I was too upset to consider what to do. With all that I had to do. Since the death-call had come, that morning. My father's body was in the hospital morgue five floors below. I had to empty the room of my father's belongings but I could not think. I could not catch my breath. The urine-odor in the room had been replaced by a frank smell of disinfectant. I thought *I won't faint, I won't be sick to my stomach.*

I was forgetting what was wrong: what was missing from the room.

My eyes were fastened on the bed. How bluntly it was now an empty bed. Stripped of soiled bedclothes. A dying man's bedclothes. A dead man's bedclothes. Mattress cover, pillowcase. (Yet the pillow remained.) It was fascinating, how not a shred of evidence remained that my father had ever occupied that bed. For weeks he'd been there, the first thing you saw when you entered the room. For weeks he'd been the reason for entering the room. But now, no. Now, he was gone. Attendants had hauled him away as a *body*, as *remains*, before the hospital had even opened for visitors.

I began to see what else was missing: the IV tube and gurney, the oxygen equipment, heart monitor. The catheter tube that had so discomfited and humiliated my father, and the urine container beneath the bed that had had to be emptied at intervals by attendants to prevent the tube backing up.

Daddy had tried to make a joke of it. A droll grim joke of past sins catching up with him. Poisons he needed to piss away, but maybe couldn't.

I shut my eyes seeing him. It seemed so preposterous, that I could not see him. As a young girl I'd often waited for him to return home in the late evening for his life was a busy and complicated life not to be contained by the house at 299 Lincoln Avenue, I'd stayed up after my mother had disappeared into the bedroom for the night, and it was like that now, shutting my eyes, waiting a second or two and then opening them . . .

The glass heart: I remembered.

Someone on the hospital staff had taken it? (I hoped it hadn't been André.) Maybe, when the attendants came to take my father's body away, the glass heart had been knocked onto the floor. Maybe it had broken. Or maybe it hadn't seemed like anything of value. Seeing it, mistaking it for a paperweight, one of those commonplace glass globes that "snow" when shaken, a hospital worker might have taken it home for a child to play with. I wanted to think this: for then I could get it back.

I would offer a reward. I would make no accusations. *Small glass heart, sculpted glass that magnifies. Missing from room 414 on or about July 11, 2004. Sentimental value purely. Please return. Reward.* My mind rushed like a runaway truck on a hill! I was biting my lower lip hard enough to break the skin.

"So sorry for your loss, Merilee . . ."

"Your father was a real gentleman . . ."

"I know, it's sad. But you have family to . . ."

". . . help you need? Just let us know."

The shock of seeing the empty bed, approaching the room almost at a run. The cardiology nurses offered their condolences. It was strange to hear my name spoken by these strangers. I'd tried to befriend them in the hope of saving my father's life, but my effort had been in vain. Now I did not want to see them. I was having difficulty seeing. I had not seen my father's body yet in the morgue, my aunt Cameron had insisted that I wait for her, for her and her daughter Beverly, they were coming to the hospital to help, and my uncle Jedah had called instructing me not to worry about financial matters, not to worry about the funeral arrangement, hospital bills, none of that, he was in charge. My task, all that I had to do, all that I had to concentrate on at the moment, was to clear my father's room of his belongings. A hospital official offered her condolences for my loss, spoke of Dennis Graf as if she'd known him, and would very much miss his presence in Mt. Olive, squeezed my hand saying if I needed assistance clearing the room, if I might be able to empty the room by, say, noon of today, this would be greatly appreciated.

I got the message. *Clear out. Fast.*

"Yes. I suppose it's like a hotel. If you stay past check-out time you'll be billed for the next day."

So quietly I spoke, and my voice so throaty and cracked, it's possible the woman didn't quite hear.

She went away, leaving me to the room. I wanted to begin before my aunt and her daughter arrived. But the glass heart was gone. I would see myself afterward in a reprise of these minutes of delirium, that look of shock, dismay, disbelief in my drawn face as if I'd been kicked in the belly and was too surprised to register pain.

"It can't be gone. No."

I was trembling now. Again I looked beneath the bed. I checked the other places, where I'd already looked. I examined the closet where my father's forlorn clothes hung on wire hangers and his terry-cloth robe hung on a hook, crepe-soled summer shoes and good leather slippers on the floor. Aunt Cameron had brought these things to the hospital weeks ago in anticipation of the day her younger brother Dennis would be discharged and walk out, a healed man.

A man with *a clean bill of health.* A man who would smile wryly with a look of gratitude *I had a close call! Now I will watch my cholesterol, I will take better care of myself from now on.* A once-proud man, a very masculine, self-absorbed man, who would be aware after this of his mortality. A man who'd had difficulty showing affection now moved to embrace his relatives who'd been anxious about him. His daughter. *Every day you were here, Merilee. I will never forget.*

I smiled at the prospect. Almost, I could hear Daddy's words.

. . . not easy to say such things but, hell. You know your daddy loves you.

I was admiring my father's clothes in the closet, that I'd never seen before. As a public man, especially while he'd been mayor and a member of the Mt. Olive city council, Dennis Graf had dressed with a certain flair. Not in the latest fashions certainly, but with taste, inclined to be conservative, in dark suits, herringbone or pinstripe, tweed sport coats, long-sleeved white cotton dress shirts worn with cuff links. Even for casual wear, Daddy had favored white shirts. Here in the closet was an Italian summer knit short-sleeved shirt, and here was a pair of pleated-front lightweight trousers, and here a seersucker jacket, and even a necktie. A necktie! Waiting for the cardiac patient to rise from his bed at last discharged by Dr. Lunbek and resume his life.

At the beginning of Daddy's hospitalization, my older Graf relatives had seemed unable to grasp the fact that Dennis might not recover. More recently, Aunt Cameron had become reconciled to the fact that he might never return home. When I'd called her that morning with the news, she'd said quietly, "Oh. Yes." A moment's silence and then, before hanging up, "It's a mercy, isn't it."

I searched the pockets of Daddy's clothes, hanging in the closet. Even the pockets of the terry-cloth robe. If anyone happened to see, I'd have been ashamed to appear so desperate. Even squatting to push my fingers up into the toes of the shoes and slippers.

Poor Merilee. Hysterical.

Donna, the young nurse who'd helped care for my father, came to sympathize with me. She'd been one of those I had befriended with little gifts. She'd had a smile for me and for my father even when Daddy hadn't been the most pleasant of patients.

When I told her about the missing item, Donna seemed vaguely to recall that, yes she'd seen my father reading with "some sort of magnifying glass" but she hadn't gotten a very good look at it and couldn't remember when she'd seen it last. "It was this size, was it?" Donna held up her hand, fingers outstretched. "I didn't see that it was a 'heart.'"

I told her it was a family heirloom. I had to find it.

The senior nurse Helen, whom I'd asked about my mother when Edith Schechter had been a nurse's aide years ago, came to see what the situation was, for by this time word had gotten out that something was missing from my father's things. When I told Helen about the glass heart she frowned and pursed her mouth guardedly. She would not commit to having seen it. But then she had not known my father very well. "Maybe it's just packed away with Mr. Graf's things?"

I said sharply, "I haven't packed anything yet! My father only died a few hours ago."

My voice was veering out of control. In another minute I would be crying, or screaming. The way these white-uniformed women were watching me, I wanted to slap their faces. They were murmuring how sorry they were, sorry that my father had died and sorry that something seemed to be missing from the room and sorry for me that I was so upset, but of course it was natural to be upset at such a time, where was my family?

Fuck my family, I wanted to say. What has my family to do with *me*.

Not knowing how they were infuriating me, Helen and Donna made a show of looking for the glass heart: Donna stooping to peer beneath the bed, Helen running her hand through my father's folded underwear and socks in the bureau drawers. I cried, "I told you! It isn't here! Someone must have taken it!" I paused, trembling. "It must have been stolen."

Now the word was said. I hadn't wanted to say it, but now it was said and couldn't be unsaid.

Donna reacted as if I'd slapped her. Hurt, and a flush coming into her face. Helen shut the bureau drawer with a slam and bristled in indignation. "I hope you aren't accusing us, Miss Graf. I hope that isn't where this is headed."

Helen went on to tell me in a voice sharp and accusatory and more forceful than my own that the hospital staff could not be responsible for things missing from patients' rooms. The hospital discouraged patients from keeping anything of value in their rooms and could not be held liable for losses. Whoever had arranged for Mr. Graf to be admitted to the hospital had agreed to this restriction. With visitors coming and going each day from seven in the morning until eleven at night, with a large work staff on several shifts, it was impossible to keep track of patients' belongings. "Downstairs off the lobby there's the lost and found, have you checked there yet?"

This was too much. I wanted to scream at the woman.

"My father's glass heart can't be 'lost'! How could it be 'lost' out of this room! It had to have been taken, it had to have been stolen, *I want it back.*"

The nurses were staring at me now, in dislike. I was losing control. I was speaking wildly. *My father's glass heart. I want it back.* These words rang strangely in my ears. I saw the flushed bulldog face of the older nurse set in opposition to me and I understood that it was a mistake to be speaking in such a way, to betray my soul that quivered with rage. I dared not make enemies of the hospital staff, if they hated me I would never see the sculpted-glass heart again.

"I'm sorry. I know it can't be your fault. My aunt is coming to help clear the room. My relatives. They can help."

Aunt Cameron embraced me, wordless in grief.

Then, a moment later, wiping her eyes as she stepped back from me to regard me critically, words came to her in a rush:

"Merilee! What on earth are you wearing?"

What was I wearing. I glanced down at myself and saw that my pleated black silk sleeveless top, that was threaded with filaments of gold fine as cobweb, purchased for me by a man friend at a chic TriBeca designer salon, was inside-out. The golden label hung conspicuously at my side. I had dressed hurriedly in the half-dark that morning, not glancing into a mirror. I had run a comb through my matted hair until it snagged on a snarl, and tossed it down. What a sight I was! What a fool. No wonder people had been glancing at me with quizzical expressions since I'd arrived at the hospital.

My aunt's married daughter Beverly, nominally a cousin though twenty years older than I was, squeezed my hand, and told me she understood: "You're upset, Merilee. It's a shock to us all, your father . . ."

I disengaged my hand from Beverly's warm moist grip. I had a powerful urge to shove both women out of the room, that I might be here alone with Daddy's things. Instead, I mumbled an apology trying not to sound sullen, for in the company of the elder Grafs invariably I turned sullen, knowing how these people had made my mother's life miserable, and I went into the bathroom to pull off the black silk top, reverse it and pull it down again over my head. I saw that my black linen skirt was at least right-side-out, and only minimally wrinkled. In the mirror above the sink, a face glared white as paste. My eyes were threaded with burst capillaries fine as hairs. Yet I'd remembered to smear crimson lipstick on my mouth, that shone like grease.

"Merilee? Are you all right?"

One of the women rapped sharply on the door. I must have lapsed into an open-eyed trance.

My aunt had reverted to her authoritarian tone, as a way of dealing with her brother's death. Maybe after the funeral she would age rapidly and give up forever her sheer stockings and high-heeled shoes but for the moment she was brusque, practical-minded. She and Beverly had come to help clear the room, they were women for whom death involved certain tasks, capably performed. When I tried to tell Aunt Cameron about the sculpted-glass heart I'd given my father, that seemed now to be missing from the room, she cut me off curtly. "That paperweight? It's here, probably. We'll find it."

Paperweight. I hated my bossy aunt, I knew myself rebuked.

Beverly said, placatingly, "It probably got misplaced, Merilee. When they came into the room, to take away your father's"—hesitating delicately not wanting to say *body*—"we can report it missing, if we don't find it. Don't be upset, honey." Beverly moved to hug me, and this time I gave in. Beverly was an attractive maternal woman in her forties, with a bosom like foam rubber, and quite a solid grip. I wanted to press my face against her, give myself up to a fit of sobbing and be comforted. Thinking *If you were a man. Any man.* A wave of sexual longing rose in me shocking as nausea.

The women had brought suitcases and durable shopping bags to fill with Daddy's things. And there was a large suitcase of Daddy's in the closet. Keeping busy, and talking constantly, was a good idea in the immediate aftermath of death, I knew. When my mother had died so unexpectedly, I'd been at a remove. Nineteen years old, away at college. Hundreds of miles away. A small liberal arts college in the southern foothills of the Adirondack Mountains. A kind of cotton batting had surrounded me. A friend had provided me with Quaaludes before embarking on the trip home in a hired car Daddy had provided. Thinking *Why couldn't she wait until the end of term.* I was vexed, and then I was very tired. I was too shocked to be upset and too sedated to cry, except at the funeral I'd been overcome by a spasm of dry-eyed weeping equivalent to dry heaves.

All that, years ago. Vague and blurred as an old movie seen on a flickering TV screen and you'd been in and out of the room during the movie, your attention on other things.

I was in the bathroom clearing out my father's toiletries. Trying not to be distracted by the glaring-pale face in the mirror. As, as a little girl, I'd been drawn against my will to peek at things that frightened and disgusted me: the sleeping snakes in the backstairs carpet, tangles of pink worms on sidewalks after a heavy rain, TV news footage of the wounded, the mangled, and the dead. My own bleeding knee, a two-inch flap of skin hanging astonishingly loose after I'd scraped it on pavement in a long sideways fall from a bicycle. In my father's study where I was forbidden to trespass there were large, heavy books of photographs, of naked women, men, sometimes even children, emaciated prisoners liberated from "death camps" in World War II, horribly blackened and blistered Hiroshima and Nagasaki atomic-bomb victims. My mother's drug-dazed face as she dropped to her knees groping for capsules spilled onto the floor in the upstairs bathroom, frantic and seemingly blind though her eyes were open and dilated . . . The temptation was too much, my eyes lifted to the mirror. I was shocked at how haggard I looked. How frightened. *You're alone now. You have that look. Anyone can have you.*

The voice wasn't my own. It wasn't my father's. A male voice, intimate and insinuating. Knowing my heart.

Hurriedly I cleared Daddy's toiletries out of the medicine cabinet: "dandruff" shampoo, "extra-protection" deodorant, long black comb, tube of toothpaste, toothbrush. What do you make of the green plastic toothbrush of an elderly man who has died! There was nothing here to keep. I swept everything into the wastebasket. The toothbrush clattered to the floor. I stooped to pick it up. Blood rushed into my head. The futility of human life rushed over me, a giant pulse near to bursting.

". . . this is it."

In the outer room, neither my aunt nor my cousin had found the sculpted-glass heart. Maybe it was missing from the room after all. "What a thing, to steal from a dying man!" Beverly said, disgusted. "It was probably an attendant, or a nurse's aide. Who knows who these people are, they don't even speak English." The meaning was *non-Caucasian.* Aunt Cameron said, sniffing, "It might have been a visitor. Dennis had too many 'friends.'"

Beverly objected, "But not a relative, Mother." My aunt and her middle-aged daughter bickered and sniped like an elderly couple.

I thought, Why not a relative?

A number of times, on my father's good days, the room had been crowded with Graf relatives whose names I'd scarcely known. I had no reason to distrust these individuals who in some cases had driven considerable distances to see Daddy, but why should I trust them? Dennis Graf's magnifying-glass heart might have found its way into someone's pocket, as a memento. Once, I'd come back to the room after an hour's break and there was my uncle Jedah conferring with Daddy, financial printouts spread across the bed, laptop computer on my uncle's massive knees, and Jedah cast me a frowning smile part-welcome, part-annoyed, saying, "This isn't of interest to you, Merilee. Why don't you go away again for a while, and please, will you shut the door?" So I'd gone away hurt and angry and at the same time re-lieved for more time away from my vigil, and when I'd returned, Uncle Jedah had left and the room was empty and Daddy lay ashen-faced and exhausted and the fingers of his right hand plucking at the paper bracelet on his left wrist as if he'd been desperate to tear it off.

Anyone could have stolen from my father. Those final ex-hausted days, nights.

The women had packed most of Daddy's clothes. Now they were examining the accumulation of cards and gifts crowding the windowsill. Potted mums, begonias, even orchids (!) whose petals were beginning to wither and fall; a massive hydrangea with clusters of showy blue petals; baskets of exotic fruits like kiwi, pomegranate, fat black Chilean grapes. There were boxes of candy in gilt wrappings, there were tins of gourmet foods and expensive mixed nuts. I'd made gifts of many of these items to hospital workers and urged Daddy's visitors to help themselves to whatever they wanted, but more flowers, baskets and candy boxes had taken their place, showy useless items that were both flattering to my father, and mocking. For Dennis Graf had long been a man of exquisite, expensive tastes, before the collapse of his health.

Aunt Cameron and Beverly scarcely troubled to confer with me, which of the potted flowers they should take home with them for the funeral and which to leave behind. I chose the blue hydrangea which was the least wilted of the flowers. I recalled that Daddy had mentioned that blue hydrangea had been my mother's favorite flower. (How improbable it seemed that my mother, who'd been so unengaged with life, as she'd been unengaged with her family, should have taken notice of these flowers at all let alone singled them out as her "favorite.")

Aunt Cameron gave me my father's watch, which had been kept in a drawer of the bedside table. "Now this is worth something, Merilee. But it wasn't stolen."

What did this remark mean? Was my aunt chiding me, for the loss of the sculpted-glass heart? I thought *Fuck you, Auntie.* But I took the watch from her and slipped it onto my wrist. It was a white-gold stretch-band with a face that gleamed with a dark undersea look. Much too large for me, swinging loose as a bracelet.

The fact of my father's death swept over me another time. It would sweep over me at such moments, unexpected, devastating. I tasted something tarry-black in my mouth.

"I know—I haven't been a good daughter. I haven't been a good person. I—"

My idiot stammered words were interrupted by the arrival of Beverly's son Brian, a lanky twenty-year-old enlisted to help us carry things down to the car. Neither Beverly nor my aunt would acknowledge what I'd said, even that I'd said anything. Brian was startled to see me, mumbling shyly, "H'lo, Mer'lee. Sorry to hear about . . ." The women fussed over him loading his arms with suitcases and bags. They were eager to leave the hospital now their task was accomplished. Aunt Cameron switched off the overhead light. I let them walk ahead. I was holding the heavy hydrangea plant in my arms. The women's constant chatter exhausted me. How the human world thrummed with such chatter, I could not bear it.

My legs were heavy as lead. The tarry taste in my mouth was becoming stronger. I could not look away from the stripped-bare bed, a metal skeleton. There was some secret about it, I could not comprehend. I began to see the man lying there: shrunken face, hollowed eyes. Yet sharp-glinting eyes, in those sockets. The breathing tube he'd hated, distending his nostrils so that the skin of his nose was waxy-white, unnatural. I heard the voice low and accusing. *Don't touch! Who are—you?*

After Lilac

This time after Lilac Jimson. When we were afraid but had stopped speaking her name.

Nor did adults speak her name any longer. Except sometimes, an exasperated mother would scold her daughter saying *Look what happened to that little gypsy-looking girl, if you aren't good it might happen to you.*

The $20,000 reward had not been given to "any party or parties providing information leading to the discovery of Lilac Jimson." The bright yellow posters bearing Lilac's smiling face had become tattered and weatherworn and had eventually disappeared. We never saw the older Jimsons, Lilac's sisters and her brother Roosevelt, near our school any longer.

(I saved one of these posters. When no one was looking I pulled it down from a wall by the Mt. Olive post office, where there were many posters and flyers. By this time Lilac's smile had begun to fade. The bright eye-catching yellow had faded and torn. Neatly I folded the poster and hid it in my room thinking *No one will ever find it here.* Except for our housekeeper no adult ever entered my room and our housekeeper would never open any drawer in my desk.)

This time after Lilac Jimson. It would last for years. When

other people began to forget, we remembered. By "we" I mean girls in our fifth-grade class at Thomas Jefferson Elementary. I mean my friends Judy, Karen, Tanya, Michele. I mean Bobbie Dyer, and Paula McKendrick who would be my closest friend in middle school. And Lizzie Foster, my closest friend in high school. We were girls who had envied Lilac Jimson before she was taken away. We had envied Lilac for her gold filling that winked when she smiled and for the glittering half-moons of gold in her ears denounced by some of our mothers as "barbaric." We'd envied Lilac shouting and laughing in gym class where she had to be first on the trampoline, first to climb the rope to the ceiling and to swing by her knees from the rings, upside-down and braids flying.

In our fourth-grade class picture at Thomas Jefferson, we were all white-skinned girls except Lilac Jimson standing far to one side who was only herself.

None of this had saved Lilac, though. Through our lives we would remember that.

There were rumors that Lilac hadn't been kidnapped, hadn't had bad things done to her and been killed, really Lilac had run away from home. She wasn't getting along with her family, so she'd hitchhiked out of Mt. Olive to somewhere far away like Florida, or Mexico. Lilac's father had been born on an island in the Caribbean called St. Kitts, maybe Mr. Jimson had arranged for Lilac to live there with relatives. Hardly a year after Lilac disappeared Mr. Jimson himself disappeared, who knew where?

I thought *We want Lilac to be alive! We don't want Lilac in the ground.*

• • •

In the bay window at the front of the house in the hours after dinner when my mother had gone upstairs to bed I tucked my feet beneath me, did my homework and waited for Daddy.

There were few headlights on Lincoln Avenue at this hour. In our neighborhood houses were large and set back from the street on large wooded lots, there was little traffic. Eagerly I glanced up whenever I saw a flash of headlights through the trees in our front lawn telling myself *This is Daddy* even when I could see that the car wasn't slowing for our driveway. *This is Daddy!* when after a long interval the next headlights appeared.

I wasn't yet fourteen. I was in ninth grade and young for my age. Skinny, and my breasts the size of unripe plums. And my nipples like unripe berries, that hurt if I touched them.

I was a nervous girl, though you wouldn't have known from my smile. I had shiny dark hair and dark eyes and my face was heart-shaped and pretty and I smiled, I was very good at smiling. It was said of certain girls already in middle school that they were "hot"—they were "sexy"—but this was not said of Merilee Graf.

I wanted badly to be liked, though. I was a girl popular with both girls and boys who brought little gifts to school for friends, classmates, teachers. I was the girl (unanimously) elected by my eighth-grade class to buy a Christmas present for our teacher and when the money collected from my classmates wasn't quite enough for a really nice present I was the girl who made up the difference with her own allowance money.

If I'd been pure of heart, I would have made up this difference secretly. But I made sure at least one of my friends knew that I'd provided twelve dollars, knowing she would pass this information on to others.

I was the girl you'd call *So sweet!*

Merilee Graf the mayor's daughter, isn't she *nice.*

Especially I liked to wait for Daddy in the bay window in winter. In slow-falling snow. Like a dream but I was awake and alert. Like a dream but my eyes were open. Most of the rooms of the house were darkened by night. Our house was so large, there was a "wing" never used. On the third floor there were servants' quarters that were poky little rooms with tiny windows, never used for Daddy did not care for housekeepers to live in. The oldest part of the house was the shut-up wing, beneath it was an old cellar smelling of oozing-wet stonework and damp earth where no one ever went. There was a new cellar with tile and white walls, a furnace room, a laundry room, a work bench and tools for Daddy though he had not much time for his carpentry hobby. Even in the new cellar there was a television set, there was a sofa and chairs but no one ever used them, in all the years I can remember.

By 9 P.M. every night, Mom went upstairs to bed. Some nights Mom and I had dinner together in the kitchen that was a large "country kitchen" with a big old wooden table where we sat at one end and a brick fireplace that was never used. Other nights, Mom had a "queasy stomach" and no appetite for food. Our housekeeper made meals for us and washed up afterward. It was rare for Daddy to return home early enough for dinner. He would eat at a restaurant or at one of his clubs. When he was mayor of Mt. Olive he had meetings in the evenings often. As the owner of Graf Imports, Inc. he had business meetings in Port Oriskany, in Buffalo and Rochester and as far away as New York City and Boston. Often he was away overnight. Most nights, he did not return home until after 10 P.M. Sometimes 11 P.M., sometimes midnight. I was not supposed to be downstairs past 9 P.M. on a school night but my mother never checked on me. Mom might scold me in a wan, listless way and sometimes she smiled in mockery to signal *I am only doing this because I am the mother.* Often while scolding me Mom did not look at me. Her eyes were restless wandering the room, her bitten-at fingernails scraped at the tender skin around her mouth.

Waiting for Daddy in the cushioned window seat I was patient, I would not give up until midnight. I would pull a brass floor lamp over to the window seat where I curled up in pajamas and a woolly robe so that I could see to do my homework or to read a book from the school library. If Daddy had time for me always he would ask what was I reading, and I could show him.

I understood that the fathers of my friends had dinner with them every night but I did not judge my father in terms of other men.

Most nights, unless he was tired, or distracted, Daddy seemed happy to see me waiting for him. He scolded me for staying up late but he might invite me into his study where he would pour himself a nightcap of his favorite Scotch whiskey, "neat." I was allowed to sniff the amber liquid that was so fierce and burning it made my eyes water and after I was twelve Daddy sometimes allowed me to sip his drink: "Just a taste, Merilee. Just wet your tongue."

Daddy was amused, seeing the face I made. But I never said no.

I loved the unexpected weight of the beveled glass in my hand, Daddy's whiskey glass that was not tall but so wide I couldn't close my fingers around it.

On a good night, Daddy would sip his drink and smoke a cigar and ask me about school. Not my friends, Daddy hadn't much interest in my friends, but about what I was learning. Sometimes I had a question for him, we could look up the answer in one of his travel books. It was special to me, to be allowed to rotate Daddy's globe of the Earth, to seek out a faraway country under Daddy's guidance. Especially intriguing were those countries Daddy had visited: Morocco, Turkey, India, Thailand, and Taiwan. Mainland China and Japan and the South Pacific islands of Malaysia.

In all cultures there is beauty, Daddy said. In all cultures there is taboo, which makes beauty possible.

I asked Daddy what was *taboo*. Daddy said it was the forbidden, that could not be spoken of.

I was eager to impress my father with schoolgirl questions and observations trying not to see how, after just a few minutes, his eyes drifted from me. Of course he was politely attentive, he was my father and seemed to love me, though at times I wondered if, waking from a whiskey-cigar reverie to hear me chattering away, he might have wondered who I was, why I seemed to imagine he was interested in my silly life. I thought *I'm not enough to interest this man. There is nothing I can do about it.*

It would be years before I realized that my mother must have had the same thought, too.

And I wondered, when? How many years into her marriage? Before I'd been born, or after?

•   •   •

This night—the night I am thinking of—because I am drinking my father's brand of Scotch, "neat" (not in my father's house which I am reluctant to enter though it is now my house, but in a bar in Chautauqua Falls in the company of a man I've only just met who'd looked, when I first saw him in the light of the juke-box, like the hospital attendant with the strong swiftly moving hands, not André, but the other one, whose name I never knew and who might have stolen the sculpted-glass heart from my father)—this wintry night in 1992 when I'd fallen asleep in the window seat sometime after midnight waiting for my father to return home, and was wakened by headlights leaping against the leaded-glass window, at first confused not knowing where I was, frightened at the sound of voices at the rear of the house, and I stood, and listened, and heard my father's voice that was slurred and angry-seeming, and the voice of another man I began to recognize as my uncle Jedah, and the men's voices were urgent and overlapping and I went into the darkened back hall to listen, thinking that something had happened to my father for it seemed that Uncle Jedah was helping my father walk, or steadying him (was Daddy drunk? I could not believe this but I hoped he wasn't ill) and I heard Uncle Jedah ask, "—come in with you, Dennis?" and Daddy said, "No, I don't need you, for Christ's sake go home." And Uncle Jedah left, I heard the door shut. And Daddy was at the closet fumbling to hang up his overcoat, cursing when it fell to the floor. And daringly I went to him, though I was old enough to know better, seeing how his eyes shifted onto me in surprised displeasure as he said, "Well, Merilee. Aren't you up late." I had not seen my father so agitated ever in the past. As if he'd been running and was short of breath and sweating. His face was mottled with heat, he was wiping at his mouth. Like an idiot I stammered some question I'd been waiting to ask him about the British Raj, it was a legitimate question related to my ninth-grade world history class except Daddy wasn't in a mood tonight to humor me saying curtly, "I think you should go upstairs to bed, Merilee. Immediately."

I was fourteen then. I was too old to be waiting up for my father. Soon after this night, my sexual life began.

II

Uncle Jedah

"Merilee."

Approximately eighty hours since Daddy died. When the hand closed about my hand. And gripping that hand, moved to grip my other hand. Not hard but firm, this grip of a large seemingly boneless and powerful hand pulsing with heat. On the third finger of this hand was a silver ring in the shape of a crude star.

The ring was a memento of a trip to Mexico twenty years before. A memento of the Mexican festival celebrating the Day of the Dead.

"My condolences, dear."

Uncle Jedah. I shuddered and would have moved away instinctively. Except for the hand gripping my hands, and an enormous thumb stroking my skin that felt raw, chafed.

Jedah Graf loomed over me, protectively. He was a massive man of six feet, four or five inches in height, weighing beyond two hundred fifty pounds. The size of him, the sight of him, always impeccably groomed and with a stiff military posture, was daunting. Jedah had to be at least fifty-two (rapidly I calculated, Daddy had once remarked on the occasion of one of Jedah's birthdays that he was twenty-one years younger than Daddy) yet his face was strangely boyish and unlined. His skin was oily-olive, unblemished. His jowls appeared muscular and resilient, not flaccid. His chin was layered, doubly and even triply, but this seemed to suggest dignity, authority. His fingernails, dwarfing mine, were neatly manicured and the backs of his big hands were covered in a dark velvety down.

"Dennis would not have objected to the funeral, I think. And the funeral cortège, I counted thirty-two cars at the cemetery— Dennis would have been gratified. Most of my plans went without error. Even the weather, that had looked ominous when we first arrived at the church."

Uncle Jedah's breath smelled of something sweet: a very minty mouthwash, or an exotic liqueur. His cologne smelled of something crushed, like rose petals.

I wanted to ease away from Jedah's moist grip but I felt strangely numb, passive. His intensity was like a thrumming vibrating presence that was alarming yet hypnotic. But we were at my aunt Cameron's house after my father's funeral service at the First Presbyterian Church of Mt. Olive and his burial in the church cemetery and so there was no escape. Through the long morning I had been many times embraced like a rag doll limp and unresisting.

"Hide behind me, dear. So that these others won't engulf you. The bulk of Uncle Jedah! No one will approach us."

I was grateful for this. I could not bear many more heartfelt condolences for my loss.

It was jarring, too, to see familiar faces of relatives, Daddy's friends and neighbors and "associates," and not to see Daddy among them. I could not adjust to his absence, in the midst of these people who'd had Dennis Graf in common.

Like Uncle Jedah. When had I ever seen this mammoth, oddly aggressive individual, except in the company of my father?

He'd had a private office at Graf Imports, Inc. where he'd been my father's most trusted assistant, a CPA with a knowledge of tax law. (Daddy had paid his tuition to the Cornell School of Business when he'd been a young man.) Sometimes, he'd even driven Daddy in the Lincoln Town Car, like a chauffeur. Often, Mom and I would hear voices in Daddy's study in the evenings and on weekends, and know that Jedah had arrived, entering the house by a side door. After Daddy sold the company, he and Jedah continued their alliance. Often in Daddy's study the men laughed loudly together. They were both drinkers, and traveling companions. *How like a son Jedah is to Dennis* it was said.

Closer than the daughter! Certainly.

Among the Graf relatives, Jedah was a loner. He lived alone in a brownstone in the historic district of Mt. Olive, overlooking the Chautauqua River. He seemed never to entertain, and he rarely accepted invitations. While Daddy had ceased traveling in recent years, Jedah Graf continued to travel abroad, and in the United States; he was a devotee of opera, and was often in New York City for performances at the Met. He visited art museums, cultural centers. He had an amateur interest in archeology, anthropology. He had a way of smiling and staring at you as if you were a specimen beneath a microscope, utterly fascinating; unless, and this was characteristic of Jedah Graf, he found you of no interest whatever, and looked through you. He was one of those Grafs who'd made my mother uncomfortable. Possibly, he'd made my mother sick: she'd suffered from "nerves"—"colitis"—"tachycardis"— "hypertension." (Eventually, Edith died of hypertension, burst arteries in her brain. At least, that was what I'd been told.) When Jedah arrived at the house, my mother slipped away like a wary cat. "Merilee! Please say hello to your elusive mother for me," Uncle Jedah would say, winking.

"Uncle Jedah." (Such a strange name! I'd long wondered what it meant, if anything.) My mother didn't think he was an uncle of mine, or even a blood relation. He was apparently an older cousin, the son or stepson or adopted son?—of a half-brother of my father's who had lived in Troy, New York, and hadn't been close to the Grafs of Mt. Olive. None of this meant much to me as a child, a kind of static came over my brain, of boredom. And none of it mattered since I'd been taught by Daddy to call Jedah Graf "Uncle Jedah" from the time I'd been capable of speech.

Say hello to your Uncle Jedah, Merilee.

Here's Uncle Jedah, Merilee. What do you say?

Now that Daddy had died, I had no reason to call the man "uncle" any longer. It was a linguistic tic I intended to break.

Jedah had called me several times since my father's death, leaving messages I hadn't returned. He'd wanted to see me, but I'd avoided him. (Escaped to Chautauqua Falls, to the historic old inn on the river. A night and most of a day in the company of a man who liked to drink and seemed to like me just enough meaning not overly much so that he'd be a problem afterward and not too little so the episode would have to feel sordid.) This morning in the cemetery I'd been aware of my "uncle" watching me closely, and I'd avoided looking at him. I knew that Jedah Graf's eyes would be brimming with emotion and that they were unusually large, very dark and oddly beautiful eyes into which in my weakened state I could be drawn to fall, and fall, and drown. Jedah's claim was *You and I, Merilee! We are the ones who grieve.*

I hadn't had a drink since Chautauqua Falls but I'd stumbled in the grass by my parents' gravesites as the minister read appropriate Bible verses over my father's shining casket. My head rang with muffled shouts no one else could hear. My eyes and nose leaked. Somehow, a mix of tears and mucus had left a whitish scum-crust on the front of my pleated black silk top, I was appalled to see.

Like dried semen, it looked. I'd tried to remove it with a wetted tissue, with partial success.

Jedah Graf was handing me a tissue now. He'd been speaking to me in an intimate, insinuating voice like lapping water. His brawny forearm, thicker than my thigh, brushed against my right breast, and his moist breath seemed to be condensing against the side of my face. How youthful his oily-smooth face was, how disconcerting that he'd incorporated certain of my father's mannerisms, a way of lowering his eyes slyly as he was about to say something cutting, acerbic, or unexpected. The modulations in his voice, too, that seemed at times taunting, at other times kindly, caressing, utterly sincere, reminded me of my father. Though Jedah was much heavier than my father, almost what you'd call corpulent, not fat, not obese, but solidly packed, rubbery-resilient like an upright python.

A python! I smiled, and shuddered.

Jedah noticed, and drew closer.

"Would you like to leave, Merilee? Anytime you wish."

I told him that I couldn't be rude. I heard myself call him Uncle Jedah.

"*I* can, dear. I can be rude. Just tell me, Merilee. I will make our excuses for us."

My aunt had invited more than forty people for an elaborate luncheon. Her house, a stately old Georgian a half-mile from my father's house, was somberly decorated with waxy-white lilies that smelled like embalming fluid. I would have liked to be somewhere else, but could not think where else except unconscious: I did not want to get drunk, so early in the day. I would have liked to be somewhere else but could not think how to get there, without passing by my vigilant aunt. I'd pulled my hands out of Jedah's grip, at least. I wiped them on the black silk trousers I was wearing, borrowed from a cousin and a size or two too large.

Jedah had ordered drinks for the two of us from a server who'd passed by offering only just white wine and sparkling water. I had only feebly protested, I couldn't begin drinking at noon! But Jedah insisted upon vodka and orange juice for me, and Scotch on the rocks, for him. "Some ordeals merit strong spirits, Merilee. The wisdom of our ancestors."

Though Jedah smiled repeatedly at me, there was something coldly sensuous about the man as if his outermost skin was a layer of tiny gleaming scales. Almost, the man moved in coils, slowly and with deliberation, a kind of reptilian grace. There was an oily, snaky glisten to his hair that was unnaturally black and thick for a man of his age. As always, for any public occasion Jedah was impeccably dressed: in a dark pinstripe suit that fitted his mammoth shoulders like a glove, a white dress shirt with a stiff, starched collar, a pewter-colored silk necktie, in his lapel pocket the tip of a white handkerchief peeking out like a tongue. I saw how Jedah's pearly, glistening teeth crowded his mouth and how striking his lips were, distinct and chiseled. I was subtly repelled by the man, yet could not move away.

A server brought us our drinks. Jedah handed me mine, I had no choice but to take it.

Jedah touched his glass against mine. Drinking, he smiled at me over the rim of his glass in a way so like my father, I was overcome by a sensation of weakness.

"Breakfast, Merilee! The purpose of the orange juice. The vodka's purpose is to make 'breakfast' palatable."

I laughed. My uncle Jedah was right. You had to make breakfast palatable, somehow.

I lifted my glass and drank. My hand trembled in anticipation. Vodka was a taste I'd appreciated, if slightly feared, as far back as high school when one of the guys smuggled a bottle of his dad's Absolut vodka out of a liquor cabinet to bring to a party.

The cemetery! I'd needed a drink then. Somehow I hadn't been thinking of my mother's grave. I hadn't expected to see EDITH SCHECHTER GRAF 1946–1997. My eyes had stared blankly. An upright granite slab, slickly gleaming, impersonal. A kind of reprimand: how many years had it been since I'd visited my mother's grave in the hilly cemetery behind the First Presbyterian Church of Mt. Olive.

I'm not your daughter!

I was no one you knew. No one you cared about.

I was Daddy's daughter not yours.

And now I am no one.

The ordeal in the cemetery had passed in a dream. One of those bumpy dreams that go on and on like driving over a rutted surface, almost I felt my teeth knocking together, a whiplash pain in my neck. Early that morning I had washed my hair in the shower but seemed not to have rinsed out the shampoo entirely, there were clots and snarls of soap in my hair. I'd brushed it fiercely, gave up and clamped it about my head with cheap plastic barrettes purchased at a drugstore. I'd remembered to smear crimson lipstick onto my bloodless mouth, that must have shone like neon.

Party girl was the look, sexy-disheveled. *Party girl the morning after.*

Another time, I lifted my glass and drank. Already I was feeling better.

". . . when I was twenty, estranged from my family and living alone in Buffalo, uncertain what I wanted to do with my life except knowing what it was I didn't want to do, your father helped me. He saw, he said, my 'potential.' When no one else did. Including me." Jedah paused, breathing deeply. A look of hurt, loss, sorrow came into his face that hovered like a moon above me. ". . . a crisis in my spiritual life, you could say. Your father helped me through it."

Spiritual life! Uncle Jedah! I laughed.

"What is amusing, dear? That there is a spiritual life, or that your uncle Jedah might have one?"

He didn't seem to be offended in the slightest. As if I were a charming little child, anything I said was delightful.

This was flattering. It was painful to recall that my father hadn't been so all-forgiving. Always with Dennis Graf there was the possibility, and more than just the possibility, of disappointing.

Jedah was saying, with an air of certitude, as if we'd been arguing and now, for all my charming obstinacy I needed to be set straight, "Our 'spiritual lives' exist whether we acknowledge them or not. By 'spiritual' I mean the voice of our innermost, secret selves, unheard by others. Christians believe, or are supposed to believe, that this is the soul, individual and immortal though immaterial as a wisp of smoke. Older and more mystical religions like Buddhism and Hinduism believe that there is no individual soul, only the soul of the universe, or the void, in which all sentient creatures including mankind participate. But all agree, this 'soul' is immortal."

"Is it!"

I laughed again, less certainly.

It was a novelty to think that my fleshy relative, who reminded me of a python, and was so clearly a lover of good drink and good food and God knows what other pleasures of the flesh, should speak of such things. Fixing me with his moist, intimate gaze, and breathing his moist whiskey breath into my face.

"Dennis believed. The secret, innermost soul beyond the gaze of others. Beyond the nets others set, to catch us."

"But Daddy wasn't religious. I don't think so."

"Not as 'religious' is conventionally understood, of course not." Jedah smiled at me, with a look of strained patience. He had halfway drained his martini without showing the slightest effect. "Tell me, Merilee: what were Dennis's last words to you?"

I said I couldn't remember.

I stammered, took a swallow of my drink, and shook my head *no*.

"Don't be ridiculous, Merilee! Of course you remember your father's last words to you."

But no, I could not remember. Really, I could not.

I tried to explain: by the time I'd left the hospital that night, the eve of Daddy's death, he'd been exhausted, not fully conscious. Whatever he'd said to me hadn't been coherent, or exceptional. He'd had a visitor that evening, a young black man named Roosevelt Jimson: did Jedah remember the Jimsons? The little girl Lilac who'd been taken from Highlands Park—

But Jedah cut me off, not to be distracted from his question: what were my father's last words to me?

"I . . . don't remember."

"Yes. You do."

"Uncle Jedah, I don't. I . . ."

"Well, I do. What Dennis said to *me,* the last time we spoke."

I was wary, this might be a trick. Jedah was staring so intently at me.

"Dennis said, 'Take care of Merilee for me. Her life is a reed thrashing in the wind, in danger of being broken.' "

" 'In danger of '—what do you mean?"

I was stunned by this remark. Since I'd been a young girl I had thought of my life in such a way, though I'd never told anyone. Not even a stranger.

"Of course I promised Dennis, I'd take care of you if necessary. If you allow me." Jedah paused, smiling. "If things work out between us."

If things work out between us. I wasn't sure what this meant.

I was Daddy's principal heir, Uncle Jedah was the executor of his estate. We would have to work together, I supposed.

By this time we'd drifted, or Jedah had herded me, into a corner of my aunt's ornately furnished living room, and from there into a sunroom-solarium that wasn't yet occupied by guests. Vaguely I'd noticed people watching us, relatives I might have wanted to speak with, old friends from high school I hadn't seen in years, but they'd been discouraged from approaching me by the massive, domineering Jedah Graf.

I heard myself tell Jedah about the sculpted-glass heart. About my concern that I would never see it again. The anger and frustration I felt, that it seemed to have been stolen from my father's room at the time of his death.

Uncle Jedah had heard about the missing glass heart, and was incensed on my account. He remembered it, certainly. "Dennis used it to read small print on some papers he had to sign. It was quite beautiful, as I recall. Dennis said it had a 'special meaning' to him because his daughter had given it to him."

I was astonished to hear this. I was deeply moved. The vodka warmed me, I'd begun to feel hopeful.

It was consoling, that my uncle Jedah took the loss of the glass heart seriously, no one else seemed to. Not the other relatives, and not the hospital officials. "It's disgusting, it's unconscionable—stealing from a dying, helpless man. Do you have any suspicions who might have taken it?"

I told him I'd been thinking obsessively about the sculpted-glass heart for the past several days, couldn't seem to get it out of my mind. Last night, early this morning, even at the cemetery my mind had been working swiftly and frantically, like wheels spinning in sand. I could imagine any number of individuals who might have stolen the heart, including individuals I'd never glimpsed, hospital workers on the night shift and unknown to me, even visitors who'd come into Daddy's room when I hadn't been around. Jedah listened sympathetically, vehement in condemning the thief: a "low-life son of a bitch" who should be arrested.

I stared at Uncle Jedah's enormous hand, balled into a fist. I felt a sensation of weakness wash over me.

I thought *He loved Daddy, too.*

The luncheon was about to begin but we resisted being drawn away. Jedah held me captive, talking. How impassioned the man was, on my account! On Daddy's account. I began to admire his girth, his solidity. His large, heavy head and the snaky glisten of the dyed-black hair; his eyes that were slightly protuberant, and intense; the glittery smoothness of his flushed skin. His mouth, that was so strikingly sculpted. I had ceased listening to Uncle Jedah's words, I was hearing only his voice that lulled and soothed, as the vodka lulled and soothed. I admired the man, that he was fleshy and abundant, while my poor father had been so ravaged in the final weeks of his life. I admired the man, that he was so much younger than my father. I saw that he was a beautiful man. A sexually attractive man despite his age.

"Merilee, what are you thinking?"

Uncle Jedah was smiling at me. I felt my face tighten, and took a step back. I told him I wasn't thinking anything.

"Just now, Merilee. Your emotions show so transparently in your face. What were you thinking?"

I laughed uneasily. I wanted to turn away. But Uncle Jedah held me still, I could not seem to move my legs.

"Were you thinking of love, Merilee?—of a lover, just now? Were you thinking, 'How starved I am, who will feed me?'"

A Dream of Butterflies

. . . glancing skyward, in my dream. And overhead a cloud of butterflies. Astonishing in their beauty but terrifying, so many! For
where there are too many there can't be enough love, God has
not enough love. God has not enough food for so many. In my
dream (which was a waking dream, a drinker's dream, the kind of
dream that drifts into the brain sweetly occluded with alcohol like
a vision from a lost world) the butterflies were large and beautifully marked like the black and yellow butterfly my father had
brought back to me from Thailand. In my dream the butterflies
were far away and yet I possessed the power to see them vividly,
even to feel the pulsing of their fragile wings. A sky of butterflies,
a darkening funnel of butterflies, tiny winged creatures in migra-
tion riding the invisible currents of the air, buffeted by wind. *How
starved, who will feed us? Where there are so many.*

Katskill Road

"Jimson."

In the night it came to me: he was the one. He'd taken my father's sculpted-glass heart from the hospital room.

In my rented Mazda in the morning I drove to 3196 Katskill Road where the Mt. Olive telephone directory indicated *R. Jimson* lived. It was approximately twenty-four hours after my father's funeral and burial and my mind was still preoccupied with thoughts of the mysterious theft from Daddy's room.

My brain felt bruised, battered. I seemed to know that I wasn't behaving rationally. *A special meaning, his daughter had given it to him.* My heart beat hard and hurting, the loss of the sculpted-glass heart was so painful.

I wasn't thinking of Daddy. I wasn't grieving, I was angry. I'd been calling the Mt. Olive hospital to ask if the glass heart had been found yet, each time routed to an administrative assistant named Elaine Lundt who'd become increasingly cool when she heard my voice. I had been able to extract from Ms. Lundt a list of the names and addresses of those numerous individuals at the hospital who'd come into contact with my father and I'd begun writing to them. My letters were handwritten, pleading and not accusatory. *The glass heart has a family, sentimental value. A reward of $200 for its return. No questions asked.*

I'd been touched by Jedah Graf's indignation on my account, the day before. Jedah thought it was a bitter thing to offer reward money to a common thief.

But I didn't care about punishing a thief, I cared only about getting back the sculpted-glass heart.

Then, I thought of Roosevelt Jimson. Unable to sleep in the hours after the funeral, the burial at the cemetery, my aunt's luncheon where I'd had too much to drink and had to hide away in an upstairs bathroom until one of my younger female relatives came to fetch me . . . In the night thinking, "Jimson. Him," and my heart kicking in apprehension.

The way Jimson had looked at me when he'd first stepped into the hospital room. His expression that was frowning and severe. He'd mumbled a greeting to me. He hadn't wanted to speak to me, he'd come to pay his respects to Dennis Graf.

I understood: Jimson would never forgive me for having rebuffed him sexually. He would never forgive me for climbing into his truck and driving with him into Highlands Park that night and yet rebuffing him. I wanted to protest *It wasn't because you are black and I am white. It wasn't even because you are poor and I'm the daughter of a rich man. It's because you are Roosevelt Jimson.*

I wondered how many white women Jimson had had. In high school he'd had white girlfriends, he'd played white girls off one another, making a display of it. So I'd heard. I'd been too young to know Jimson, then.

I wondered how many white women Jimson had made

scream, and thrash, and clutch at his muscled back with their fingers.

Rubbing his stubbled jaws against soft flesh. Taking delight in the abrasion, the hurt.

And so it seemed to me he must have taken the glass heart, in his arrogance. To show that he could take me, a part of me, if he wanted.

I shut my eyes. I could see Roosevelt Jimson closing his fingers over the glass heart on my father's bedside table. Amid the clutter of Daddy's things it would have looked small, inconsequential. In a quicksilver movement, when no one was looking, Jimson slipped it into his pocket.

Oh God. I had to hope he'd kept it, otherwise I would never see it again.

"Never go there, Merilee. Never alone."

So my mother had warned me. When I'd been a little girl. After Lilac Jimson. Those years.

Now I was driving through Highlands Park, on my way to Katskill Road. I was driving on Ravine Road which cut through the large sprawling park at the southern edge of Mt. Olive.

It was a day of warm gusty winds, a low cloud ceiling. A smell of imminent rain. My eyes kept glancing skyward, looking for thunderhead clouds. I was trying not to feel anxious. Or maybe it was hopeful I was trying not to feel.

If I encountered Roosevelt Jimson . . .

If I dared speak with him . . .

Highlands Park was a county park of hundreds of acres

adjoining a state wildlife sanctuary in the foothills of the Chautauqua Mountains. Most of the area was densely wooded. The ancient glacier-gorge that cut through Chautauqua County at a north-by-northeast slant cut through the park, too, diagonally. Only when I'd become an adult driving her own car did I realize how the ravine, as it was called, cut through Mt. Olive linking certain of its neighborhoods. From the air you'd have been able to see how the affluent old residential neighborhoods of Lincoln Avenue and Summit Boulevard, built on a ridge in northern Mt. Olive, were connected to Highlands Park by the deep, meandering ravine that ran behind some of the properties. (Like ours at 299 Lincoln Avenue, though the ravine was not visible from any room in our house.) In theory, you could hike the ravine from Highlands Park to our house, a distance of about two miles, but in reality only intrepid hikers would attempt such a hike. The ravine was at least twenty feet deep in many places and strewn with enormous boulders. There was no hiking path. In summer there was a shallow stream that trickled through the ravine, after the spring thaw and after heavy rains the stream rushed swollen and discolored with debris, suddenly dangerous. There were stories of hikers who'd almost drowned in the ravine, in flash floods. As a little girl I'd been cautioned never to play in the ravine beyond the edge of our property and so I had not. Unlike some of my girlfriends, I wasn't a tomboy. The risks I would take, when I was a little older, were of other kinds.

Sixteen years since Lilac Jimson had disappeared from Highlands Park and it didn't look, from the road, as if much had changed. Maybe the park was looking shabbier. Maybe there were more overflowing trash cans, more areas of burnt-out grass.

Where there'd been a rose garden, now there was an asphalt parking lot.

At this time of day, the park was mostly deserted. A few children in the wading pool. A few teenaged boys playing softball. Few cars on Ravine Road headed south.

Black boys, in oversized T-shirts and shorts drooping from their hips, stood at the edge of the road, smoking cigarettes. Their eyes lifted to me as I passed.

Mt. Olive and vicinity were overwhelmingly Caucasian. The relatively few people "of color" in the area, who'd moved to Mt. Olive from Port Oriskany, Buffalo, Rochester, were the more visible.

My Graf relatives were not racists. Certainly, Daddy hadn't been a racist. Yet, I'd grown up hearing these adults speaking of "Negroes"—"blacks"—with a certain intonation of voice meaning *not-us, different-from-us.*

I'd never thought of how Lilac Jimson must have felt, the only "gypsy-looking" girl in our fifth-grade homeroom. Lilac and her older sisters seemed so self-assured. Their brother Roosevelt had been one of those older boys you looked away from quickly, not wanting to make eye contact.

As a girl I'd known instinctively to look away from a boy like Roosevelt Jimson. The color of his skin had nothing to do with it.

I wasn't a girl who wanted to be hurt. If I behaved recklessly at times, these were calculated times. By my twenties, I'd become a skillful hunter. I preferred men who were older than I was, who were grateful for my attention; who were likely to adore me even before we had sex. (And sometimes it wasn't necessary to have sex.) As a college student I'd gone out with boys who were attractive but shallow, I could count on to mean nothing to me emotionally. If they called me after a night of partying together, or if they did not. If they remembered me, or if they did not. Sometimes I was astonished when one of these boys fell in love with me, as if a comic strip character had come suddenly to life claiming he was real, he had a soul.

No. I couldn't believe this.

Daddy didn't approve, my men friends were unknown to him. He'd have liked me to marry the son of one of his well-to-do business associates, and live here in Mt. Olive. He'd seemed to sense something secretive about me, a willfulness belied by my daughterly manner, my pretty face. He was shrewd enough to know that I was drawn to men, but he couldn't have guessed how I avoided being involved with men I knew I couldn't control.

I had no strong sexual feelings, generally. Sex was obliteration, forgetfulness. Fleeting and impersonal like an appetite for eating or drinking: easily satisfied and when satisfied easily forgotten. There was a kind of purity in this, I thought. Where emotions didn't intrude.

I was twenty-six, I'd never loved any man. Almost I might have thought that my mother had counseled me *Don't trust, Merilee! Don't feel. Don't make my mistake and love a man, your heart will be shattered.*

Of course, Mom hadn't spoken to me in such an intimate way. Not once, not ever.

Slowly, at twenty miles an hour, I was driving through the park on Ravine Road. My heart beat hard as I approached the picnic grove from which, it was believed, Lilac Jimson had been abducted. Beyond a softball field, beyond a graveled parking lot, the picnic grove that had been so thoroughly searched by police and rescue workers . . . Even in daylight it exuded an air of secrecy, mystery. The trees here were enormous oaks, stately old trees that dwarfed the picnic tables and benches. I braked my car and stopped, and stared. Lilac's sisters' accounts of what had happened that evening had been confused and inconsistent but the general belief was: the eleven-year-old had been left behind.

Sixteen years. Lilac's body had never been found. No one had ever come forward to explain what had happened to her. If it was known, by anyone living, what had happened to her.

Lilac would not have gotten into a stranger's car, I thought. She'd been the kind of girl to run from a stranger. But if the abductor had been someone known to her, someone she'd trusted, who had seen her alone on foot at the side of the road, at night, and had stopped to offer her a ride . . .

Hundreds of people, mostly men, had been questioned by the police. Very likely, the abductor had been among these. Yet he'd slipped through the net. No one had suspected him, for Lilac herself would not have suspected him.

I drove on. Across the plank bridge above the gorge, beneath overhanging trees. A barely visible stream passed below hidden among rocks and stunted trees. Lilac's abductor would have taken this route, I thought. The quickest way out of Highlands Park and into the countryside beyond.

But the outskirts of Mt. Olive had been built up in recent years: gas stations, fast-food restaurants, discount stores, automobile dealers and strip malls. I felt only repugnance for this debased landscape, I hated to think that Roosevelt Jimson lived out here. He was such a proud man. He was such an arrogant man. *Don't try that white-girl shit with me. Like you don't know Jimson.*

Several miles south of Mt. Olive, the landscape became more rural. Here were small wood-frame houses, mobile homes on cement blocks, roadside produce stands and shuttered farmhouses on properties for sale or lease. I was having difficulty locating 3196 Katskill Road, slowing to stare at numerals scrawled on mailboxes. I had never known anyone who lived in the countryside south of Mt. Olive which extended through Eden, Wyoming, and Cattaragus counties to the Alleghany River and the Pennsylvania border a hundred miles away. It was a harsh, beautiful landscape of steep glacier hills and vast sweeping vistas across which cloud-shadows raced like the shadows of predator birds high overhead.

Finally, I located 3196: a ramshackle farmhouse partly covered in asphalt siding, beside a gas station and convenience store called Cappy's. There were no farm buildings remaining. The acreage had long since been sold. In the front, mostly grass-less yard of the farmhouse were derelict autos, one with a FORE SALE sign propped up in its windshield. A dark-skinned woman was sitting on the front steps of the farmhouse veranda, with a small child. I saw that the woman was young: bosomy, good-looking, in shorts and a tank top. It came over me with the force of a blow to the stomach, Jimson was probably married. In my vanity, in my desperation somehow I hadn't thought of this.

No wonder Jimson had fixed me with a look of sexual disdain: "I don't need *you.*"

I parked in Cappy's dirt driveway, went inside the small convenience store and bought a Diet Coke and a package of marshmallow cookies from the proprietor, an older black man with short, nappy, mist-colored hair. I wondered if this was Cappy: this fattish, friendly, grandfatherly man baring gold-capped teeth in a smile. "Here y'are, ma'am. Thank *you.*"

I thought I saw the faintest trace of Roosevelt Jimson in the man. The angularity of his face, the shape of the nose. But Cappy, if this was Cappy, was much darker-skinned, thicker in the torso and shorter-legged than Jimson.

And much friendlier.

Outside, I stood hesitantly glancing toward the buxom woman sitting on the veranda steps. She was in her early thirties, with a broad nose, wide nostrils, thick heart-shaped lips. Her features were slightly oversized, as if crayon-drawn. She wore snug blue jersey shorts and a tank top that fitted her lush body like a swimsuit. She was noisy with laughter, teasing her little girl in a pink pajama-looking top and a drooping diaper. I smiled at the child, I called over, "How old is she? She's darling."

Like the proprietor in Cappy's, the woman was immediately friendly. It seemed natural that we began to talk. I was admiring of the child Buena who was two, shy and yet alert, with curious shining-dark eyes. Her skin was a creamy cocoa, beautiful.

Impulsively I asked the woman, "Are you Selena Jimson? Lilac's sister?"

This was a mistake. At the sound of "Lilac," the woman's smile faded.

"Yes. I'm S'lena. How'd you know Lilac?"

Both mother and daughter were staring at me now. The mother's eyes were brooding, suspicious. I told Selena what seemed to me true: "Lilac was in my fifth-grade class at Thomas

Jefferson Elementary. Lilac was my friend." I paused, faltering. "I missed her. I still think of . . ."

Selena busied herself with her little girl, with a kind of sullen tact giving me time to recover. Or time to return to my car and drive away. Speaking so abruptly of Lilac had been a mistake. Selena and her little girl had been happy together and I'd intervened. The two-year-old knew nothing of Lilac who would have been her aunt if only she'd survived. It was an error to bring up the dead in the presence of such innocence.

I held out the package of marshmallow cookies to Buena, as if to make amends. The little girl glanced at Momma and Selena nodded yes. "What do you say to the nice lady, Buena?" Buena, taking a cookie and beginning to nibble at it, mumbled thanks.

Eyes like Lilac's. Thick-lashed, shining-dark.

Selena was one of Lilac's older sisters, who'd been named many times in the media. Selena, Marvena: teenaged sisters who'd "forgotten" their younger sister in the park and didn't remember her until hours later, when it was too late.

Selena Jimson, Marvena Jimson. Commentators who hadn't felt comfortable chastising Alina Jimson, the grieving mother of the lost girl, had come down hard, and repeatedly, on the sisters. I had heard that both girls, stricken with shame, never returned to school afterward.

I told Selena I was sorry to have brought up the subject. I'd just come home for a short while, visiting. "My father's funeral."

How strange, how formal and final-sounding: *my father's funeral.*

Selena's eyes were large and expressive, sympathetic. She murmured she was sorry for my loss.

I heard myself say, naively, "I don't live anywhere near Mt. Olive any longer. But I think of Mt. Olive often, of being a girl here. I still think of . . . I miss . . ." My eyes filled with tears. Selena and I were staring at each other, as Buena prattled happily.

Selena heaved herself to her feet, sighing. For such a warmly fleshy woman she was unexpectedly short. In a lowered voice she said, "We miss that girl, too. But she's gone, for sure."

I said, "Sometimes we'd hear—I mean later, in high school— that Lilac had been 'seen' somewhere. Florida, or—"

Selena shook her head irritably: "Bullshit."

Now Selena wanted to talk, taking care that Buena wasn't listening closely. She told me how crazy it made them, Lilac's family, hearing things like that "just made up out of nowhere" suggesting that Lilac had run away, or run off with a boyfriend. A girl of eleven! Or that she'd been taken as blackmail by drug dealers in Port Oriskany because their father had owed them money. "Any kind of nasty thing, to make us feel ashamed. Like, we ain't feelin' bad enough, Lilac gone, and the police never findin' her, folks got to make up lies to hurt us worse, and not just white folks, either. Oh, no."

I touched Selena's hand, which was trembling. I took hold of her hand, closing it in my own.

Her fingers, strong and warm, clasped mine. It was a strange moment, unnerving. For I wasn't one to touch another person, and certainly not a stranger. My instinct was to shrink from being touched, not to touch another. I was trembling too, frightened. For the feeling came so strong.

I told Selena what seemed only true: people hadn't meant to

be cruel, but to be hopeful. It was a primitive way of wishing that Lilac was still alive.

"If she was, see, it would mean . . . might mean . . . the rest of us, too . . ."

I broke off, confused. I didn't know what I was saying. Selena swiped at her eyes with the forefingers of both hands, in a gesture oddly like my own. Buena was clutching at her mother's plump dimpled knees, peering up at us. What were we talking about so earnestly! I was thinking how utterly trivial my search for the sculpted-glass heart was. How petty I was, to be obsessed by it.

I asked about Selena's family.

She told me that Marvena was living in Port Oriskany, and had three kids. Her mother had died a few years ago. And there was her brother Roos'velt, living here with her and Buena and Uncle Cappy, at least some of the time. "Roos'velt is his own man, nobody can keep track of him. Always been that way."

Selena spoke of her brother with an air of exasperated pride.

I told her that I'd lost contact with Roosevelt in recent years. Vaguely I would lead her to think that I'd known him at Mt. Olive High School. She would have to wonder if we'd gone out to-gether: if I'd been one of Roosevelt Jimson's white girls.

"Roosevelt came to visit my father in the hospital just before my father died, but we didn't get to talk."

"Roos'velt came to see your father? How'd he know him?"

I told Selena my father's name. I spoke of the fellowship to the police academy. I saw how Selena blinked at me, impressed. "Mr. *Graf?* Your *father?*"

Evidently I wasn't looking like a rich girl from Lincoln

Avenue right now. Sweat-tendrils of hair in my face, and my face pulpy-white as bread dough.

"Your father? That was mayor of Mt. Olive a while back? He was a nice man, for sure! Gave money to older students, like Roos'velt, that'd been messin' up their lives, to go back to school." Selena frowned, deeply moved. "Aw honey, I guess I saw it on TV, the other night. 'Dennis Graf.' I saw that, I was real sad."

I thanked Selena. But it was Jimson I wanted to know about.

Selena said vehemently, "That man! He ain't doin' so well, that's a fact. Half the time he ain't here, nobody knows where in hell he is. See, he's living here right now, payin rent on this place, he's got a job at the mall, security guard at Wal-Mart 'cause he's suspended from the police force, got in trouble with the court for 'excessive force' last September and it wasn't the first time. My damn brother, he's got a temper, bad as our Daddy. He had some trouble as a kid, got expelled from school, but made it up afterward and was doing O.K. people thought, then he got his way paid to the police academy up at Rochester, there was only five applicants picked and Roos'velt was one, from Mt. Olive, I mean, and he did real well there, and came back here and was hired by the Mt. Olive police, and they liked him, but he's got this temper, he got so fixed on that certain kind of man, you know, that goes after children—'ped-o-fill.' That kind. Roos'velt and his partner picked up one of 'em and was takin' him to the station, but something happened and Roos'velt hurt him kind of bad, the fucker had to be taken to the hospital where his jaw was found to be broke, and some other things. Maybe you heard about it, there was a lot in the paper and on TV. This guy he beat up on was a black guy, lucky for Roos'velt or it'd been worse. On account of

Roos'velt was just a rookie, see. Those fuckers, like that, they don't deserve to live, like the one who . . . you know, took Lilac. But Roos'velt got suspended with no pay and havin' to take some 'therapy'—'anger management'—so he told them fuck it, he ain't gonna take that kind of shit. But we're pissed at Roos'velt, too: he graduated from the Academy and was so proud, and we was proud. All of us that's left. So Roos'velt fucks up, and almost gets sent to jail hisself. Shit."

I was astonished to hear this. My head rang with the reiterated *Roos'velt* like a musical chord. I loved to hear Selena Jimson speak of *Roos'velt* in that way of exasperated pride, as only one who loved him could speak of him. Though I'd heard what Selena had said about his job I had to ask her, to hear her say again that he was a security guard at Wal-Mart.

"He don't carry no gun, though." Selena laughed, stooping to pick up Buena in her arms. "Just as well, Roos'velt had a gun, he'd of killed somebody by now."

Security Guard

At Wal-Mart, at a discreet distance I sighted him.

At Wal-Mart in the Northland Mall. Into which until now I had never stepped.

Unmistakably, the man was Roosevelt Jimson. Tall, solidly built, burnt-gingery-skinned. In his early thirties. Inclined to frown. With facial whiskers bristly-repellent as a giant black hairy spider clutching at his jaws.

Jimson was stationed in the check-out area. If he hated his job, if he believed that it demeaned him, who should have been a law enforcement officer carrying a nightstick, flashlight, revolver and two-way radio and handcuffs attached to his shiny leather belt, and not just a crackling walkie-talkie, he didn't show it.

Wal-Mart! It wasn't my scene.

When I shopped in Manhattan, it was in very different kinds of stores and always, you can be sure, in smaller stores. Wal-Mart was enormous as a warehouse. This relatively new store at the mall commanded an entire corner of the mall and what looked like acres of parking space. It felt as if such a vast space must generate its own wind currents, which tended (on a midsummer day) to be refrigerator-cold. I saw that Jimson's uniform was a crisply ironed pale blue short-sleeved shirt and trousers of a dark-blue serge. His footware looked like combat boots. If I'd dared to come closer, I could have made out the identification on his brass badge and braided epaulettes, that mimicked that of a police officer's.

So Jimson, a young black recruit in the predominantly white Mt. Olive Police Department, had been suspended for using "excessive force" against a suspected pedophile. I hoped he hadn't quit police work permanently; hoped he hadn't insulted his superiors so he'd never be hired back.

I didn't want to think so. I wanted Jimson to be something more than a Wal-Mart guard for the rest of his life.

"Just like you, Jimson! 'Fucking up' a good thing."

I shared Selena's exasperation. I was angry with Jimson as if we'd been quarreling.

"Disappointing my father, too. 'Dennis Graf' who'd helped you . . ."

Seeing Jimson now, I'd come to doubt that the man had stolen anything from my father's hospital room. That sudden fantasy of mine, lifting abruptly out of a dream of emotional/sexual yearning, had faded in the fluorescent-lit clarity of the gigantic store. *Girl, what'd I want with your crap! Not a thing from you.*

In my fantasy, I'd imagined confronting Jimson. My heart had begun to beat with excitement at the prospect. But now, in the crowded store, peering at Jimson from my hiding place in Kitchen Appliances, I understood that that wasn't going to happen: I was stone cold sober.

"Fuck 'sober.' But I'm not going to drink for *you.*"

This was so. God damn if I would drink for Roosevelt Jimson, or with him. I would not.

Spying on Jimson, I was intrigued to see how indifferent he was to women shoppers who occasionally glanced at him. In fact, he was indifferent to his surroundings. From time to time he glanced at children passing by him, followed a child with his eyes for a short while, but that was it. His stance was stiff, guarded, military-straight, yet essentially mechanical, detached. It would have required an act of sudden disequilibrium, a violation of the dull routine of Wal-Mart shopping, to rouse the man to alertness, and action.

And then, three girls drifted past Jimson. I'd been vaguely aware that these three had drifted past Jimson just a few minutes before. They were sexy-skinny white girls, high school age, with eye makeup, glittery nose rings, pierced eyebrows and softly rounded tummies partly exposed above low-slung jeans. I saw how the girls were hoping to snag the good-looking black man's eye, how they nibbled at their lower lips in slow smiles, shivering, giggling, glancing at one another, and at him; finally disconcerted when the black man with the bristly goatee ignored them.

I drew back as if I'd been rebuked, too. Suddenly I was desperate to escape before Roosevelt Jimson saw *me.*

Sexy

I've said that I did not have strong sexual feelings and mostly that was so. When I felt most excited, sexy-palpitating, was when I bought gifts.

My pulse quickened. Adrenaline kicked, flowed.

After I fled Wal-Mart, I shopped in the children's department at Macy's, humming under my breath. There was a peach-colored cotton playsuit that reached out to me sharp as a fishhook sinking in my skin *Here! Buy this.* I heard myself telling the sales clerk, "She's two years old. My little niece. My sister's daughter. She's darling." In a fever of spending I bought the playsuit, a pink cap with a visor rim, a white summer knit cardigan sweater, a T-shirt imprinted with yellow ducklings, and a pair of fuzzy red bedroom slippers. The sales clerk was a motherly woman who beamed at me: "What a nice aunt you are. You and your sister must be very close."

I was trembling with happiness. There is nothing to make you feel so good about yourself as buying gifts for a child.

"I think we are, yes. My sister Selena and me. We're the only sisters in our family."

I handprinted the bunny gift card TO BUENA JIMSON. I handprinted the address label:

SELENA JIMSON
3196 KATSKILL ROAD
MT. OLIVE, NEW YORK 13028

I pondered how to sign the card. If I signed *Merilee Graf,* Jimson might learn of it, and I didn't want that. If I didn't sign the card, Selena might be suspicious.

I decided just to sign *Lilac's friend from 5th grade who hopes to see you both again sometime.*

Forbidden

Just a sip, Merilee! Just wet your tongue.

It wasn't a drinking day. It was a gusty-clear blue-sky day to make you feel good about yourself even if you didn't feel good about yourself.

Three days after my father's funeral I called the hospital to ask about the sculpted-glass heart. Hearing the stiffness in Elaine Lundt's voice informing me what I already knew: "I'm afraid that your father's 'glass heart' hasn't yet been found, Miss Graf. But we are continuing to look for it and to make inquiries among the staff."

Are you! I wanted to mutter something sarcastic/obscene and hang up, loudly. But I only just thanked the woman and hung up quietly.

Three days after my father's funeral I hauled the blue hydrangea plant in my rented car, to plant at the old house. The cobblestone house which I was to inherit. Halfway up Center Street, a steeply hilly street that intersected with Lincoln Avenue on what was known as the Ridge, I began to swallow compulsively. In a state of apprehension I turned onto Lincoln Avenue. My neck was aching from the strain of my stiff posture as I leaned forward to stare through the windshield at the aged plane trees lining the avenue, that with their tall columnar trunks and wanly peeling bark and spiky leaves beginning to curl with summer heat looked like illustrations in a child's storybook.

Daddy had taken to grumbling that the neighborhood on the Ridge was going "all to hell" which was an exaggeration of course. But some of the plane trees were dying, and others had been so severely trimmed they resembled immense upright stumps with some sort of leprous skin condition. Most private properties were still beautifully maintained but others were showing their age, like ours. Those massive houses—of fieldstone, granite, brick, limestone, cobblestone—built in the early decades of the twentieth century were beginning to be taken over by commercial interests: directly across the street from our house, a showy neo-Georgian mansion once owned by a prominent Mt. Olive banker was being converted into THE ELMS: A LUXURY RETIREMENT COMMUNITY. Also on Lincoln Avenue was an elegant old brownstone housing DE SALES PHOTO STUDIO and DUDLEY MARKS SCHOOL OF BALLET. The largest residence on Lincoln Avenue, like ours designated as an historic landmark, was now THE SOTH CENTER FOR THE ARTS.

"I can give away my inheritance, too. I don't have to live here."

I spoke aloud, defiantly. I might have been arguing with my father, or my uncle Jedah.

I parked my car at the curb. I walked up the driveway. This was eccentric behavior. Maybe I was being watched. I was carrying the bulky hydrangea. Its dyed-looking petals were mostly brown by now and many had fallen off. Its leaves were beginning to brown and curl, too, though I'd watered the plant carefully.

(Maybe I'd overwatered it?) I set the plant down on the front walk, peering up at the house. *Such a beautiful house! Such a— striking house—*

Everyone said such things to us, but you could see, in plain daylight, that the house was ugly. There is something too dense and heavy about cobblestones. They seem to glisten sullenly as in a perpetual cold rain. Windows in such old houses are smaller than windows in newer houses and so these, recessed in the massive facade, had a look of dim, hooded eyes. And the heavy slate roof like a low sloping forehead.

The house was fronted by a granite portico and, inside a circular drive, a three-foot marble-faun fountain no longer functioning. Broken tree limbs, a spray of dead oak leaves lay in the fountain. Tall thistles had begun to push up through cracked paving stones. In a recent storm, trees and ornamental shrubs had been damaged. I stood dry-mouthed and swallowing, staring at the bay window where splotched sunlight reflected on the panes like a childish face.

Just a sip, Merilee! Just wet your tongue.

Where I'd waited for him. For Daddy. A man I'd known as Daddy whom I'd waited for, with such childish anticipation.

I left the hydrangea plant on the walk, went around to the rear to a storage shed where gardening tools were kept, rusty old implements that must have been decades old. I selected a spade with a wooden handle. My hands were soft, I wasn't accustomed to this sort of physical exertion, and had to smile at my intentions, or my naïveté. No one in our family had been a gardener: not Daddy, certainly not Mom who'd rarely left the house. I remembered being astonished visiting girlfriends' homes and seeing their mothers tending to flower beds and gardens: was this what women did? Normal women?

I'd made my naïveté into a sort of gift, to offer to people.

Girls, boys. Men. *Oh Merilee! How funny you are.*

I struggled to plant the damned hydrangea plant, in a weedy rose garden at the front of the house. By the time I'd finished, my soft girl-hands were aching and I'd broken two fingernails.

All this while, I'd been uneasily aware of the house. Like a collapsed monument it seemed to me: a mausoleum. Those heavy, ugly cobblestones!

I fumbled for the key to the house, in my pocket. Aunt Cameron had given me the key, which was attached to a plastic key chain upon which someone had printed GRAF 299 LINCOLN. For a moment I'd thought that I had lost the key, but I had not.

As a college girl living away from home and returning for short visits, I'd seemed always to be losing my key to the house. And later, in my many moves, in my numerous travels, I'd lost keys.

I had this key, though. I gripped it tight. It took patience to open the front door for my hand was shaky and the lock was old. As soon as I stepped into the foyer, I thought *This is a mistake.* But I didn't turn away. I shut the door behind me. My nostrils contracted against the peculiar airless-earthen odor that had begun to pervade the house in recent years, since Daddy had shut off most of the rooms.

To conserve energy, he'd said.

I'd wondered if there was some reproach here. My aging, ailing father who'd always been so distant to his family, hinting now that he was lonely. Living in the grand old family house, and lonely. But he'd insisted upon remaining here, hadn't he? I had not thought it a good idea to suggest to him that he might find other, smaller quarters more comfortable for a single man of his age.

I was standing in the cavernous living room. Light was splotched here, the leaded-glass windows were in need of washing. I had forgotten how forbidding this formal room was, how as a girl I'd tried to avoid it. The furnishings were late Victorian, said to be "museum quality" but not very comfortable. The carpet was massive, lead-colored; on the walls were clouded mirrors, Chinese scrolls, shadowy shelves of carved jade, ivory, teakwood. The most striking object was the Steinway baby grand piano, though its beautiful burnished-red finish was covered in a film of dust and its ivory keyboard was closed. I felt a pang of guilt. I didn't suppose that the piano had been much played since I'd given up my piano lessons, after years of misery.

I'd been ten when I began, sixteen when I'd quit. It was amazing to me to recall how, though I'd been on the whole such an obedient, docile daughter, I had complained to my mother about the lessons.

I hate this old piano! Hate hate hate being cooped up in this house!

I hate having no talent for the piano, and people pretending that I do.

My father had been the one who'd insisted on my taking lessons, as he'd done long ago, on that identical piano. My mother hadn't cared in the slightest.

I didn't approach the piano now. I could see, from where I stood, at a distance of about fifteen feet, my bright red *Classic Piano Favorites* lesson book. Virtually each page of the book had been annotated in pencil, by my piano teacher Mrs. Deiter, or by me. Each page represented approximately the degree of frustration, misery, and suffering you'd experience having a wisdom tooth removed with an only partially effective anesthetic.

Sixteen when at last I'd been allowed to quit, on a fretful Saturday in June 1994. When in sudden disgust with me, Daddy had said *All right.*

The sight of that book, and of the piano, filled me with a sudden revulsion. I felt that I could not breathe, I would have to break a window.

Hate having to pretend . . .

Beyond the living room was a formal dining room (there were two dining rooms, neither much used) with a faded floral-print wallpaper and more heavy, carved mahogany Victorian furniture. I had few clear memories of meals in this room, at the long gleaming table, for we'd usually eaten (my mother and me, or just me) in the kitchen. A few times, in celebration of one or another special occasion, a holiday, a birthday, Graf relatives had joined us to fill up the table of some ten or twelve seats, Jedah Graf had smiled puckishly lifting his wineglass in a toast to my cringing mother . . .

To Edith! Our lovely hostess.

Of course, my mother had little to do with these lavish meals. They were prepared by a cook or a housekeeper, following Daddy's instructions.

On the mahogany breakfront, as elaborate a piece of furniture as the Steinway piano, was a nineteenth-century German clock with ebony hands stopped at 4:44 of a long-forgotten day.

I wondered what I'd eaten, at those meals! I'd been a finicky eater as a child, with an easily upset stomach.

The dining room chairs, spaced about the table precisely, unmoved for years, had unnaturally high backs, like thrones. I seemed to recall sitting in such a chair, my toes barely touching the floor.

There came Daddy's startled voice *Edith, where are you going?* in the quicksilver moment before it shifted to annoyance *You're being rude to our guests, you must know* and in my mother's wake as she'd hurried from the room without a backward glance *My wife hasn't been well, please excuse her.*

Mostly, we did. We forgot her, too.

Across the corridor was Daddy's study. Out of habit, I'd been keeping the door shut. For always when I'd been a girl, the door had been shut. I pushed it open now, shyly. No one could be inside but I felt hairs at the nape of my neck stir in apprehension.

This was ridiculous, for I'd been in Daddy's study several times in the past weeks. He'd sent me here to bring him books, magazines, papers from his desk. I had found the sculpted-glass heart in one of the desk drawers, to bring to him.

Now that Daddy was gone, this room that had been his place of refuge had a melancholy cast. It was still a beautiful room but it had been invaded by death. There was pathos to the objects here, as there'd been to Daddy's left-behind toiletries at the hospital. The exquisitely carved jade horse on his desk top, said to be a fifteenth-century Chinese antique; the golden, blank-eyed, life-sized head of a twelfth-century Tibetan Buddha; Indonesian masks on a wall; the elaborately patterned Chinese carpet, more foot-worn than I remembered. There was the hefty leather sofa where I'd sat as an adoring girl, looking toward Daddy behind his desk; there were brass lamps, faded-gold brocade drapes at the windows, strands of cobweb hanging from the elegant white molding overhead. There was the globe beside Daddy's desk, he'd set to rotating with a magical touch of his fingertips.

I would keep the globe, I thought. I wasn't sure what I would do with the rest of my father's treasures.

The Victorian desk with its numerous compartments and pigeonholes, gilt-handled drawers, inlaid pieces of teakwood in geometrical patterns reminiscent of Islamic art. I had tried at one time or another to open all the drawers in this desk but several were locked and there was no key that I could locate.

Behind the desk was a filing cabinet with several drawers, the lowermost locked. And there was a door in the wall, between shelves of books, that opened into a closet, also locked.

I tried the door of my father's liquor cabinet and was surprised that it opened. Here were dusty glass shelves containing numerous bottles, glittering and inviting: whiskey, bourbon, vodka, gin, single-malt Scotch. Beside the near-empty bottle of Scotch was a glass that looked as if it hadn't been washed in some time.

I shut the cabinet door, quickly.

I supposed that the locked drawers and the closet contained business documents, income tax files, old letters. Daddy had a safe deposit box in a Mt. Olive bank, that hadn't yet been opened. I didn't think these might contain anything of interest to me. Like the shut-off, airless rooms of the house, that included the entire third floor, the servants' quarters and the old, earthen-floored cellar, I had little interest in exploring.

A wave of dread passed over me. *You don't want to know.*

I contemplated the floor-to-ceiling bookshelves. Daddy's priceless books. Many were antiques, first editions. Most were oversized, with leather bindings, gilt lettering on their spines. These had been forbidden to me as a girl (for what if I tore or stained a page? dropped a book, broken its spine?) except when Daddy looked on as I turned pages marveling at old maps, reproductions of artworks, photographs of places and people so strange to me, they might have been on other planets. Daddy had seemed to like me asking him questions if they were the right questions.

Had he been to these places? I asked.

Daddy laughed and said yes, of course.

Would he take me someday? I asked.

Daddy smiled strangely and said someone would take me, though maybe not him.

"But why not, Daddy? I want to go with *you*."

I spoke aloud, now. My voice was soft with wonder, not reproach.

A few times in Daddy's study, when I'd dared to come in here by myself, uninvited, I'd pulled a forbidden book from a shelf to quickly leaf through the pages looking for—what, I didn't know.

Sometimes, shocked, my eyes widening in alarm, I found it.

Now, an adult woman, whom very little that was likely to be found in a book could shock, I pulled down one of my father's oversized art books from a shelf near his desk. It was a massive volume of sacred Hindu shrines, taken by a British photographer in the 1920s. The title was stamped in red: *Images of God.* I leafed through thick parchment pages of photographic plates, pausing to stare at the more striking, "exotic." Here were shrines to such Hindu deities as Krishna in his incarnation as a warrior, the dancing destroyer Shiva, the great mother/devourer Kali. I stood staring at a vividly colored photograph of what appeared to be fantastically entwined serpents in bas-relief above a shrine to the creator god Brahma, in Khajuraho. When I looked more closely, I saw that the serpents were actually human beings, naked men and women with blank, sensual faces in a writhing chain of copulation.

In fact there were numerous "erotic" plates in the book. These were set incongruously amid stark, disturbing photographs of appallingly crowded streets in Calcutta, Benares, Delhi. Here were beggars, maimed and emaciated children, elderly men and women shrunken as corpses in rags on filthy pavement as others, in brightly colored Indian clothing, walked by oblivious of their suffering.

I shut the book, that was repulsive to me. I shoved it aside.

I knew: the Indian erotic images were considered beautiful, even sacred. Yet the sensual art was so casually mixed with the other, of human suffering. That was the obscenity, not the sexual.

Daddy had smiled, mysteriously. *In all cultures there is taboo, which makes beauty possible.*

I was at the liquor cabinet, which matched the exquisite in-laid teakwood of the desk. The glass was in my hand as if I meant to wash away the smudged fingerprints but instead I only just wiped the rim of the glass on my sleeve. My heart beat quickly, with daring.

Never had I tasted single-malt Scotch though I'd known several men of refined, expensive tastes who preferred it to any other liquor.

This brand was Dalhousie. A heavy brown bottle that was about one-quarter full. I poured just a little, perhaps an inch, into the scummy glass.

I saw Daddy's bemused eyes on me. *Just a taste, Merilee!*

That was all I would take: just a taste.

I coughed. The dark liquid was so potent, my mouth and throat so suddenly aflame, almost I could taste nothing.

I waited for this sensation to pass. For I knew it would pass.

I returned to Daddy's desk, and again tried the locked drawers.

No. You don't. Don't want to know.

Glass in hand, flamey sensation in my mouth, throat, spreading into my veins, I examined other areas of Daddy's study looking for drawers, cabinets, secret compartments. There was a teakwood table beside the leather sofa with a drawer that seemed to be locked—but no, it was only just stuck, and I tugged it open.

Inside was a cache of handwritten letters, dating from the 1980s. I pawed through them, selecting one written on a perfumy lavender stationery, dated March 3, 1988.

Dear Mister Graf

This is to thank you for your kindnesse. As others have said you are a good Christian man. If it had not been for the Graf Scholarship to allow my son Benjamin to enroll at Chautauqua County Tech there would be no future for him with his "juvenile record" though that is long behind him. My deepest grattitude and prayers, sincerly yours

Irene Bagley
744 Upper Ridge Rd
Mt. Olive, NY

All the letters in the teakwood drawer were like this, handwritten expressions of gratitude. I swallowed the last of the single-malt

Scotch in my glass, and went to pour another, very modest quarter-inch. I drank, and I read. A flame passed through me, deeply into me. My eyes filled with tears. My father had touched so many lives, changed so many lives, he'd been such a good, generous man. I drank, and I began to cry. I wiped at my eyes with both hands. Why was I crying? What had I expected to find among my father's things?

Cellar

Wishing she would die! die! die!

I was thirteen. In eighth grade. Calling Mom in my girlish uplifted voice.

In the cellar, I found her. The old earthen-floored part of the cellar where no one ever went.

Through the house, calling Mom. Hopeful balloon voice you would never associate with fear. "Mom? Where are you? It's—"

As if I'd have to identify myself. *It's Merilee.*

Your daughter, Merilee.

Because she wasn't upstairs. Not in my parents' bedroom and not in the room where (I wasn't supposed to know this, maybe) my mother actually slept and not in the bathroom where (door shut, locked) she sometimes hid, being sick.

And she wasn't downstairs. Julia, our housekeeper, shook her head quickly No! no idea where Mrs. Graf was.

In the garage, my mother's car, oddly mud-splattered, was unmoved.

How many days, weeks. Since that car had been moved.

How many days, weeks. Since Edith Graf had left the cobble-stone house at 299 Lincoln Avenue.

Ohhh if I hated my mother, if I wished the woman would die,

you wouldn't have guessed from the sweet girlish voice lifted in alarm, not in dread, anger, rage.

. . . daughter Merilee, remember? Me?

I went into the basement, switching on the overhead light. Our sleekly modern basement, a "family recreation room" with pale beige stucco walls and a rich russet-red Mexican-tile floor, state-of-the-art TV screen, CD player with an elaborate speaker system, fieldstone fireplace in which no fire, for as long as I could remember, had ever burned, attractive sofas and chairs in which no one, for as long as I could remember, had ever sat.

As if Edith Graf would be down here!

I pushed open the door to the laundry room, adjacent to this room. I pushed open the door to Daddy's "work room"—a carpenter's bench outfitted with numerous tools, a hobby Daddy hadn't had time for in years.

I pushed open the door, unpleasantly warm to the touch, to the furnace room where two furnaces thrummed with heat.

Where! where! where are you! At last shoving open the door to the old cellar, the earthen-floored cellar where no one ever went.

And the door jammed against something, someone.

This was the "historic" cellar. While the rest of the house had been remodeled, expanded, modernized, this dank, cave-like space had been left untouched. I'd been told that, long ago, there had been a cistern in this part of the cellar, and a large fruit closet: a place where canned jars of preserved fruit, jams and jellies were kept cool through summer heat. As a little girl I'd peeked into this cellar only once. I had no interest in exploring it.

No one ever went into the old cellar except there, huddling in her bathrobe on the floor, bare legs twisted up beneath her, was my mother. Even as she shrank from me, her eyes glared up at me. Her greasy hair hung in her face. Her breath was a hot sour rotted-hay smell.

When I tried to touch her, Mom pushed away my hand.

When I squatted beside her, to help her to her feet, Mom pushed me away with a grunt.

No no no don't touch. Go away I'm sick.

Heiress

". . . And to my daughter Merilee, to be held in trust until her thirtieth birthday, a sum of one-quarter of my estate as well as my property at 299 Lincoln Avenue, Mt. Olive, New York. Said estate to be duly executed by . . ."

The inheritance would compute to approximately eight million dollars, I was being told. Until my thirtieth birthday, by which time the eight million would have increased substantially, I would receive a fixed payment annually, to be administered by the executor of the estate, Jedah Graf.

They were looking at me expectantly. My Graf relatives, and a number of strangers. We were all beneficiaries of Dennis Graf's estate. But I was Merilee, the heiress-daughter. You would think that I had won a lottery, or lightning had struck me splitting my skull in two.

Was I expected to respond, I think I must've been. My tongue was gluey-numb. My breath stank like rotted hay. I had not slept well the previous night. I did not expect to sleep well this night.

Hearing words read from a document in a flat, pedantic voice. The voice of Dennis Graf weirdly distorted, diminished in the mouth of the somber Mr. Weiden.

I'd walked to the law office of Krampf, Hudgkins, O'Nan & Weiden in the courthouse district of Mt. Olive, a block from the brownstone where Graf Imports, Inc. had once been. In Mr. Weiden's office, I sat apart from the others, not in a mood to chat.

I was wearing Daddy's watch, loose on my wrist as a bracelet. It was a heavy watch, with a white-gold stretch-band and a large oval face. It was a Swiss watch, Genève. While the lawyer had been reading Daddy's will, I'd been studying the watch face. Its primary color was an undersea plum-black that shone like a gem. Upon this background was a constellation of pale gold lines, like filaments, most of them very thin but some that thickened in strategic places to indicate numerals: not the actual numerals of a clock face like 1, 6, 12, only the symbols of such numerals. You would have to know the design of a clock face perfectly or you could not "tell" time with so stylized a watch.

The silence had become awkward. Mr. Weiden had evidently asked if I had any questions. I didn't know how I felt about a stranger calling me "Merilee" as if he knew me.

I said, "I think—I want to give away the house. I don't think I will live in that house."

My father had left endowments to a number of charitable organizations: the Disabled Children's Fund of Western New York, Chautauqua County Caregivers, Chautauqua County Literacy Volunteers. I thought that one of these could have the property. I could not imagine a private family living there, as we had done.

My Graf relatives were not happy with this announcement. My uncles, my aunts, several older cousins. They had disapproved of me for a long time and now they had reason. Aunt Cameron said, with admirable restraint, "If Dennis had wished to donate that beautiful house to charity he'd have done it himself in his will. But he didn't, he left the house to *you*."

In the way of an adult defending a confused and exasperating child, Jedah Graf intervened: "Of course, Merilee will do what she thinks her father would have preferred. And she has plenty of time, since the will won't be probated for months."

Months! I wanted to laugh aloud in childish relief.

Months was an unfathomable quantity of time, in my zombie state. It might as well have been *infinity*.

In the corridor outside Weiden's office, the man I no longer wished to call "Uncle Jedah" waited for me, smiling. Somehow it had happened, it was "Uncle Jedah and Merilee" in collusion, bonded together against the dull Graf relatives.

Drinking hard liquor at Aunt Cameron's house. Stirring looks and murmurs of disapproval.

Jedah walked me to the stairs. Jedah spoke with chiding authority.

"Merilee, you haven't been sleeping. Certainly, you haven't been eating. You know how Dennis would be upset, seeing his beautiful heiress-daughter looking anemic. We will have to do something about it, eh?"

I was frightened of Jedah Graf. I felt a physical revulsion for Jedah Graf. Even as I admired his strength, his demeanor. His subtly modulated voice like that of a trained singer.

I laughed, weakly. I did not say *yes* though I did not say *no*.

Since my aunt's luncheon, I'd managed to avoid Jedah Graf.

I had a memory of his having said something very strange to me in the moment before my aunt came to touch my arm and announce firmly that lunch was being served.

Walking beside Jedah Graf, I felt child-sized, insubstantial.

I didn't want a ride back to the house I was staying in, I'd planned on walking. Yet somehow it happened, Jedah Graf was driving me: "We have much to discuss, dear! Your life, you must know, has taken quite a dramatic turn."

I'd been in contact with a friend in Manhattan. A drinking friend, and a man. Vaguely I had promised I would be returning in a few days, and wanted very much to see him. It was late, beyond 2 A.M. Really, I wasn't sure what I had said. In the whitish light of midsummer in upstate New York, my faltering nocturnal words evaporated. If Jedah had known what I'd been plotting, he'd have waved it all away like shooing flies.

". . . your life, which you must guide carefully. No more drifting, careening, skidding about . . . though, God knows, and Uncle Jedah knows, how attractive such a life can be . . ."

Uncle Jedah sighed, and smiled. He had only to touch my arm lightly, to guide me in his direction. Not to the front walk but to a sidewalk, smooth-worn aged brick, leading to a parking lot.

I had liked it that, in the lawyer's office, the fussy Weiden had several times deferred to Jedah Graf. The man was princely in his very corpulence. There were folds of pale flesh at his neck like a nobleman's ruff. As always he was impeccably groomed and dressed, in a summer suit of a lightweight material, dove-gray stripes. His face was handsome and ruddy, his eyes intense. Nothing in my father's will had been a surprise to him, of course.

Jedah always drove new-model, expensive cars, so it was no

surprise to see that his current car was a bronze-green Porsche. Gallantly he helped me climb inside, shut my door for me, and came around to fit himself behind the wheel in the way you would fit an arm—a husky, sinewy arm—into a snug sleeve. I held my breath, that he would fit. Staring at his thigh, the man's flesh straining against the fabric of his trousers, only a few inches from my own.

How luxurious, the interior of the Porsche. Smelling of new leather. And the windows dark-tinted. Bucket seats close together, driver and passenger reclined together in sudden startling intimacy.

As soon as Jedah turned his key in the ignition, a passionate soprano voice filled the interior of the car. "Callas is too much for us, for now." Jedah switched off the radio. (He subscribed to satellite radio, he explained. Opera, classical music. What we'd been hearing was *La Traviata*.)

The car was in motion. It was too late for me to turn the handle of my door and escape. I fumbled with a seat belt, like a good girl strapping herself in.

In his princely way, Jedah drove along narrow Mt. Olive streets. Through the historic district, onto wider, busier Main Street, with an air of barely disguised impatience for slower, less competent drivers in ordinary vehicles. His voice was confiding, subtly coercive: "I knew, Merilee, that Dennis was leaving your inheritance to you in trust, and I knew about the house, of course. What may not be known is that the will we heard read this morning was drawn up years ago, after your mother's death, somewhat hurriedly. Dennis had meant to update it, but never got around to doing so. He'd never quite realized that he would—would not—be returning home." Jedah sighed, and laughed, sadly.

I was staring at Jedah's hand on the steering wheel. A massive hand. Yet the fingernails were manicured. His shirt cuffs were spotlessly white. I supposed that Jedah Graf's clothes had to be custom tailored, even his shirts. I remembered my father speaking of having several suits custom-made in Hong Kong, when I'd been in high school.

Yet Jedah carried himself with unexpected ease, like any large creature assured of its strength and authority. I'd liked it how in Weiden's office, Jedah had intimidated my sharp-tongued Aunt Cameron.

Why was the woman so critical of me! As she'd been critical of my poor mother.

". . . only after I'd told him how urgent it was. Before your poor mother died . . ."

We were driving along the river. Jedah hadn't asked where he should take me, and I hadn't thought to tell him.

". . . a shock to him, of course. And not only emotionally but you might say intellectually. Because, unbelievably, Merilee, your father had refused to draw up a will for years. I think he was so charged with life, so fixed upon a future in which he would continue to prevail, he lacked a sense of mortality . . ."

I was distracted by Jedah's scent, so intimate and cloying: the crushed-petal cologne, the oil on the starkly black-dyed hair. I had the uneasy sense, like an intimidated child, that Jedah Graf could read my mind.

". . . a proposition to make to you, dear, which I think you will find reasonable. Since your father's will was prepared in haste, and he hadn't had time to . . ."

Jedah's words lapped over me like warm water. I sensed that there was something Jedah Graf wanted from me, wanted very badly, that perhaps he wasn't telling me, yet I seemed to know that it would be better for me, not to know. *Here is a man who wants to protect you. Be grateful for him.*

I wondered if my mother had misunderstood him. Maybe he'd been very fond of her, too.

". . . intended to renovate the house substantially. The slate roof is in need of repair, the furnaces need to be replaced, and that old earthen-floored cellar, Dennis had intended to wall off, completely. Your father was such a perfectionist, he'd have been horrified to know that he would pass away, and the house would come to you, in such a state of disrepair . . ."

I was staring out the window. For a startled moment, I thought we might be driving into Highlands Park. But Jedah continued past the intersection with Ravine Road.

". . . while your mother was alive, of course. The upset of having carpenters, roofers, masons on the premises would have been too much for her sensitive nerves. Poor Edith!"

When I'd been informed of my mother's death, I had not known how to respond, either. A zombie consciousness had slid onto me like a mask through which I could breathe, shallowly. Friends in Mt. Olive and at college had seemed to feel sorry for me and so I'd tried to match my feelings in response to their expectations. Like nitrous oxide at the dentist's: you retained enough consciousness to know that you were supposed to be feeling pain, but you weren't feeling pain.

For a long time, I hadn't much feeling except a compulsive need to yawn. In Jedah Graf's car, I was feeling a convulsive twitch in my jaws.

"... sleepy, dear. Rest your head on my shoulder if you wish."

Jedah spoke tenderly. I shrank from him stammering no, I wasn't sleepy. Only just a little tired.

Adding, in a near-inaudible murmur, "... Uncle Jedah."

Uncle Jedah. I'd vowed to break the linguistic habit, but I could not seem to. I'd been conditioned by more than twenty-five years of speech.

It was the churchyard behind the First Presbyterian Church of Mt. Olive we were headed for. Jedah drove the Porsche along the narrow graveled lane as far as he could; then we left the car, and climbed the remainder of the way. By the time we reached the top of the hill, Jedah was short of breath. Yet his color was rich, ruddy. He seemed to be enjoying the exercise. "... a surprise for you, dear. I hope it meets with your approval."

I saw that my father's grave marker was in place, at the head of the fresh-tilled grave. The smooth-faced granite stone was an exact match for the one Daddy had chosen for my mother.

For a long tremulous moment I stood staring. I saw how Jedah glanced sidelong at me, in the way of an adult who hopes a child will appreciate a gift. I saw how beautiful the grave markers were, obviously expensive but not ostentatious. DENNIS WILLIAM GRAF 1931–2004. EDITH SCHECHTER GRAF 1946–1997. On the one, a layer of fresh earth that appeared to have been seeded with grass. On the other, lush grass that had recently been mowed.

"... I will buy your father's house from you, Merilee. I will take it off your hands. We will have it appraised by a realtor, and whatever the price, I will give you $50,000 more." Jedah's breath still came quickly. He was dabbing at his forehead, that gleamed as if with miniature jewels, with a white cotton handkerchief. "You are so young, my dear! An 'historic' property would be burdensome to you, like an extra, dead appendage."

I began to cry, hiding my face in my hands. My ravaged face, that wasn't so pretty now. Delicately, Uncle Jedah drew away. I knew he was close by, I knew he was watching over me, but he didn't touch me, didn't try to restrain me, allowed me to cry, for as long as I had tears.

From the cemetery, we drove to Uncle Jedah's house.

The Seduction

"Eat, eat! We must bring you back to life, Merilee. *He* would wish it."

In a large, heated bowl, garnished with fresh parsley and croutons, was a rich creamy ginger-colored soup. Its smell was overpowering. I lifted a long-handled, slender soup spoon to my mouth, and tasted.

Reluctantly I'd come with Jedah Graf to his town house. Reluctantly I was sharing a meal with him. He had seated me in a patch of sunlight in his chilly kitchen, where with the fond, frowning precision of a mother tending to her newborn infant, he ladled soup from a tureen into both our bowls. I'd tried to explain that I wasn't hungry, the prospect of eating had no appeal, yet as soon as I stepped into my relative's kitchen, smelled the soup he'd been keeping in a warm oven, as soon as I began to eat, I became ravenously hungry.

He'd prepared the soup early that morning, Jedah said. He loved to prepare food as the sun rises.

I swallowed a spoonful of the pungent, creamy soup. By now I was trembling with hunger. My hand lifting the spoon began to shake and Uncle Jedah steadied it with his hand, as if his gesture were the most natural thing in the world.

"It's good, eh? Can you guess what it is?"

We were sitting in an airy alcove of a compact, gleaming kitchen. We were surrounded by windows on three sides, overlooking a rear, walled garden. Jedah Graf's town house was an eighteenth-century brownstone on Stuyvesant Square in Mt. Olive's oldest district. I'd had an impression of polished hardwood floors, brightly colored scattered carpets, oversized contemporary furniture in stark colors. The windows were unadorned, with only just white louver shutters. There were works of art—carved, sculpted, painted, woven—like my father's North African and Asian things, but fewer of them. Where the atmosphere of our house on Lincoln Avenue was crowded and claustrophobic, the atmosphere of Jedah's town house was spare, subdued. It was rumored among the relatives that the eccentric bachelor Jedah had spent more than a million dollars renovating the three-storey brownstone that fronted on a narrow cobblestone street in a semi-commercial district of Mt. Olive. Except for my father, no one had ever been invited to visit Jedah in this house.

I felt privileged. And uneasy. I'd expected Jedah to have a housekeeper, but there appeared to be no one in the house except us. From time to time a telephone rang, but Jedah ignored it.

In the background, an opera was playing at a low volume. I heard only teasing peaks and ripples, muffled crescendos and isolated chords.

Jedah Graf was a cook! As soon as we stepped into his kitchen, he became bustling and exuberant. Removed his coat, removed his gold cuff links, rolled up the sleeves of his white cotton dress shirt to the elbows. It was a shock to see such ham-sized forearms, brawny as a laborer's. The incongruity of my middle-aged relative's neat-manicured nails and the pelt of thick dark hairs that covered his arms.

I offered to help Jedah with the meal but he shooed me away without a word. In his kitchen he was practiced and efficient; his movements were choreographed, even ritualized; you could see how he abhorred the thought of an outsider intruding, however well-intentioned.

"Sit, sit! Eat! While it's hot! *Can't* you guess what my soup is?"

Steam from the soup lifted into my face, clouding my vision. I was so very hungry, my mouth flooded with saliva. I worried that I would shame myself in front of my fastidious relative, by beginning to eat voraciously.

It was like sex, such hunger. Sudden, astonishing. You don't realize you have been starving. You don't realize how close you are to losing control.

I thought the soup might be cream of mushroom? Yet it had a sharper, spicier taste.

"It's chestnut soup. Delicious, eh?"

It was. It was delicious. I told Jedah I'd never tasted anything so delicious. Probably, I hadn't known there was such a soup as chestnut.

Jedah laughed. As if my naïveté pleased him.

"But there is every kind of soup, Merilee. All things organic can be liquified, distilled, reduced—'souped.'"

I laughed, and shivered. I fumbled for my water glass.

With the soup, Jedah served an arugula, watercress, walnut and endive salad with egg lemon dressing. He served heated hard-crusted French bread, sparkling water in a brilliant blue bottle, and what he called a "dark, fruity" pinot noir. The soup bowls,

Jedah said, he'd brought back from Tuscany: they were made of beautiful glazed pottery, in bright colors. The large salad plates were Swedish in design, of a pure crystalline glass. The water goblets were large, and heavy; the wineglasses, with twisted stems, were delicate as works of blown glass. I was very thirsty as well as hungry but I knew to drink only sparkling water, not wine.

For a man of his size, with an obvious, exuberant appetite, Jedah ate and drank with mannered restraint, like one accustomed to observing himself. Across from me at the table (elegantly designed in black walnut, set with silverware in a graceful, contemporary style wholly unlike our ornate inherited silverware in the house on Lincoln Avenue) he loomed above me like a cumulus cloud spreading into the sky, unnervingly close.

"I used fresh chestnuts, of course. Roasted, peeled and puréed with carrot, onion, celery; fresh-ground pepper and nutmeg, and dried thyme. Chicken stock and heavy cream. And another, crucial ingredient, dear: can you identify it?"

To avoid my relative's close scrutiny, I shut my eyes. I was thinking that he'd intended to bring me back here all along; he'd known before our meeting at the lawyer's office that I would return here with him.

He would have known, too, that I would walk with him in the cemetery, I would burst into tears at my parents' graves. Reluctant to enter his house on Stuyvesant Square yet I would enter it. I would sit at his table, and eat his food.

The night before, and the night before that, I'd sprawled on my bed without removing most of my clothes, only just kicking off my shoes. I'd avoided eating. I'd avoided eating with others. At 10 P.M., I'd driven to House of Chung, a storefront take-out near the train depot and, in my car in the darkened parking lot, devoured a gluey sugary dish with tiny prawns like insects, spooned onto gummy white rice. Later, unable to sleep, I staggered into the bathroom and stuck a finger down my throat and threw up.

"You see, you must take better care of yourself, Merilee. Now that you are an 'heiress.'" Jedah winked, smiling. He shifted his weight in his chair so that it looked as if he were about to rise over me. "If you do not, your years of youth and beauty will pass even more swiftly than otherwise."

I had not been able to identify the mystery ingredient in the soup, and was hoping that Jedah would forget about it. He began telling me about his "romance" with food and drink, that dated to his first trip abroad, with my father, in the spring of 1975 when they'd traveled to Rome, Naples, Sicily, and Morocco. Back home, he'd taken scattered courses in cooking, one summer at the Culinary Institute of America in Hyde Park ("You've heard of it, dear? No?"); he'd had isolated lessons with master chefs in Paris, Rome, Bangkok, Tokyo. "None of the Grafs knows about my secret life as a cook except your father, who didn't approve, I think. Dennis took a dim view of his 'right-hand-man' squandering time and energy on anything other than Graf Imports, Inc."

Jedah laughed, and sighed. For a moment, Daddy's presence was almost palpable.

Without asking me if I wanted more, Jedah ladled soup into my nearly empty bowl, and into his own. I was still hungry, and grateful. In the lawyer's office I had held myself apart from the others, not wanting to speak with them, but really I felt like a stray, starving cat, grateful for any small kindness.

"I love to watch you eat, dear. This is our first time. A scrawny starving thing you seem to me, in need of nourishment."

I laughed, blushing. Uncle Jedah could read my thoughts! When I'd been a little girl, I'd taken for granted that any adult could read my thoughts.

It was crucial then to be *good*. To be perceived as *good*. As I wished to be perceived by my sharp-eyed relative.

Jedah went on to say, as if this was the subject we'd been discussing all along, that it was a "wise, reasonable decision" for me to sell my father's house to him and let him take on the "anguish of responsibility" of renovating and repair. He knew what Dennis had intended to have done to the house and the adjoining garage, and with whom he wanted to work among local contractors. "When the work is completed in a few years, I will make over the deed to one of your father's favored charities, in need of permanent housing. An organization that wouldn't be out of place on Lincoln Avenue, now that zoning restrictions have been changed. I'm thinking perhaps the Disabled Children's Fund. Dennis would be pleased with that."

"But . . ."

I tried to protest. Why couldn't I give away the house, myself? In Daddy's name? Why did Jedah have to be involved? There was something here I wasn't comprehending, some leap in logic. My brain wasn't functioning clearly. My tongue felt thick. Jedah cut me off laying a warm heavy hand on my arm.

"Merilee, I've explained! Your father was a perfectionist who would not have wished for anyone, especially not his daughter, who knows so little of home ownership and financial responsibility, to take possession of that property in the state of disrepair it's in. A 'landmark' house, grown frankly shabby. As you know, Dennis shut off much of the house after your mother's death and became a virtual recluse. Such valuable antiques and works of art in that house, and yet the roof, the electrical wiring, the plumbing, the furnaces—all need replacing. It was at my insistence that Dennis drew up a will at all, in 1997. He had thought of it as only just expedient, not permanent. He'd named you his principal heir when he'd had no intention of dying. 'Merilee at age thirty'—that had seemed to him, at the time, a distant prospect, since you'd been just nineteen when the will was drawn up. Do you understand?"

Uncle Jedah's eyes. I had been seeing them all my life, or wishing not to see. So dark, intense. And the warm heavy hand on my bare forearm.

"I . . . I don't know, Uncle Jedah. I . . ."

Jedah listened patiently, allowing me to falter. I had no idea what I was saying. I could not remember what he'd asked me. I felt the floor tilting beneath my chair. My impulse was to grab at the man's hand, to clutch hard.

". . . explained, the will won't be probated for months, haven't I? Why should you be burdened with property ownership, if you intend to give the property to charity? You can't imagine the responsibility, dear. Especially involving a 'landmark' house. Financial and legal details. Dealing with the contractor. All this, I mean to spare you. I am the executor of your father's estate, this is my duty, but more importantly, dear, I am your friend. I am the only person in Mt. Olive who cares for you. I'm thinking that you will not want to remain in Mt. Olive, surely? Your New York friends must be impressed, now you're an heiress?"

I couldn't follow all this. I wasn't sure of Jedah's tone. I told him I didn't have friends. I'd broken off with people I'd known in New York and had begun to forget them.

"And your lovers, too? You're forgetting?"

I lowered my eyes, embarrassed. Lovers? Had I lovers? Or only just men I'd had sex with, occasionally? Here in Mt. Olive, in Jedah Graf's kitchen, I could not have said their names.

I shook my head mutely. Jedah nodded, pleased. He liked it that I was forgetting my past.

" 'Before Daddy's death and after.' I think I see. You may reconstitute yourself. You are an intriguing young woman, Merilee, if somewhat shallow and undefined. I'm thinking now that even if you allow me to take the burden of that house off your hands, you might remain a while in Mt. Olive."

I'd eaten most of my salad, and drunk most of the sparkling water; without knowing what I'd done, I had taken several swallows of the fruity pinot noir. There was soup remaining in my bowl, which Jedah helped me eat, for I'd become strangely sleepy, and could barely lift my spoon to my mouth.

My head was so heavy! I wanted to lower it onto my crossed arms on the table. I seemed to be falling forward, into darkness. I might have upset the soup bowl except Jedah, lithe on his feet for such a large man, came quickly beside me to hold me, to cradle my limp body in his arms. "Merilee! My dear niece. Let Uncle Jedah take care of you."

In my sleep I was smiling. I was so very happy. The emptiness inside me had been filled. I was warm, I'd stopped shivering. The rank rotted-hay taste was gone. The taste of my own sour breath, in my mouth. I could recall only the delicious creamy liquid, that brought me such peace. Thinking *He loves me, he will protect me. This is proof.*

Waking alone, in an unfamiliar bed.

It was dusk. Deepening to night. Against a window facing my bed, what appeared to be a wall of shadow.

The window was tall and narrow and without adornment except white louver shutters, which were partly closed.

I had slept so deeply! A dark delicious sleep through the day, at least nine hours. I realized that I was naked, in clean linen sheets. Bathed and smelling of bath powder like crushed rose petals.

I fumbled to switch on a bedside lamp. My father's wristwatch had been removed from my wrist and lay on the table, propped so that I could see the time: it looked like 8:30 P.M. My clothes lay neatly on a nearby chair. My shoes neatly positioned in front of the chair as if I'd stepped out of them.

Naked! In this place I didn't know. Not anyone's bedroom but what appeared to be a guest room: a sparely furnished room of white walls, a pedestal mirror, a chintz-covered chair in bright poppy colors.

He has seen me naked. He has bathed me. The knowledge, that should have filled me with revulsion and anger, left me profoundly grateful. *Like a baby, bathed.*

Jedah Graf had fed me, and bathed me. He must have carried me upstairs, sleeping. He undressed me, he lowered me into warm bathwater and bathed me. His touch must have been gentle, for I had not wakened. The ends of my hair were still damp.

No one had been so gentle with me, that I could remember. Maybe, many years ago, before the terrible change came upon her, my mother. Or maybe not.

I lay very still in the bed, that felt sumptuous to me. In my sleep I had a habit of locking my arms together over my body, hugging my rib cage as if to keep myself in place. For, as a girl, I'd worried that I might fall up into the ceiling. I gripped my arms tight, beneath my small hard breasts. I felt my heart beating as if at a distance, as if the possession of another, subject to his whim.

I seemed to be hearing music, from below. Voices—a baritone, a soprano—lifting in a duet. I could not determine if it was a duet of love, or of struggle.

Vaguely I could remember, as if it were the sweetest of dreams, being lifted in a man's arms. A man's thick brawny arms. And the intimacy of his blood-tinged face, his breath. A blackish smell of hair oil. If I had not wanted to be lifted, and carried, if I had not wanted to be stripped of my clothes, and laid naked into bathwater, and bathed like a baby, I had not the strength to protest.

This was a fact: my body that had been feeling battered and aching, as if with a perpetual flu, felt now totally rested. My skin that had been feeling chafed felt now healed. And the deep delicious sleep left my brain feeling healed.

I swung my legs out of bed. There was the shock of my nakedness, again. Quickly I retrieved my father's wristwatch, and slid it onto my wrist. I was relieved to see that a robe lay over the arm of the chintz-covered chair, to spare having to put on my clothes, my underwear, that smelled of my body and would have to be laundered.

I wrapped myself in the robe, which was a kimono: a beautiful garment made of a rich, dark purple silk. The material was soft against my skin. It was a little large for me, falling to just below my bare knees. I tied the sash. I was not yet steady on my feet, after my stuporous sleep; I felt as if I'd been drugged, or had had too much to drink. In the fleeting instant before I turned the glass handle of the bedroom door the terrible thought came to me *I am locked in, I am his prisoner.* But the door opened easily; to mock my childish fear.

I stepped into the hall. Even upstairs, the floor was polished hardwood. My bare toes curled. As I approached a staircase, I could hear the music more clearly: opera, probably Italian. I smiled to think that all the men I'd known had had their music. Always it was special to them. Rock music, jazz, classical music. Even country-and-western, bluegrass. Even New Age. Music was syncopated noise to push away silence. I'd known men who listened to heavy metal rock on Walkmans while working out at the gym, or working at computers. I'd known a man who, aging into his forties, was desperate to own every record, CD, bootleg tape of Bob Dylan. I had not known any man intimately who liked opera. I was not naturally drawn to opera but perhaps I would learn.

I made my way down the stairs, to what appeared to be the second floor of the town house. Now I heard the phone ring below, and Jedah answering.

Why I did what I did next, I don't know: instead of continuing down the stairs to the first floor of the town house (warmly lit, I could see the sweep of the carpeted stairs from above),

I made my way stealthily along the second-floor hall, past closed doors. Behind one of these doors was a linen closet. Behind another door, a small office with a computer, printer, fax machine. Behind another door, a bathroom. And behind the door at the far end of the hall, a large, handsomely furnished bedroom.

I switched on the overhead light. White walls, skylight, bright woven carpets like floating peonies, white louver shutters at the curtainless windows. The bed was enormous, covered in a silk brocade spread, a dozen small pillows positioned on it. On a pedestal table was a carved jade horse, like my father's Chinese horse. And here and there on polished surfaces were similar carvings, Asian or Indian. But on the walls were large ink drawings of what appeared to be Japanese court ladies, or geisha girls, of another era: their high-piled black hair, exaggerated facial and sexual features, the way in which they coyly held their fans against their bodies, suggested erotic art.

On the table beside the king-sized bed was a stack of oversized books: the erotic art of Gustav Klimt, Egon Schiele, Picasso. And other books, by lesser-known artists. A gigantic television screen faced the bed, there were numerous videos and CDs shelved close by. I thought with a kind of childish triumph *Pornography! Uncle Jedah's secret.*

I came farther into the room. It was fascinating to me, to have entered Jedah Graf's bedroom. Here, the scent of crushed petals was noticeable, and the underlying smell of hair oil. I knew, if I opened a closet door, and smelled Jedah's clothes, the scent would be overwhelming.

I was not offended by erotic art, nor even by pornography. I didn't think so. I had never known a man, or a boy, not drawn to such images. Some had wanted me to see pornographic films or videos with them. Like many women I wanted to think that pornography was essentially harmless as a way of blocking the thought that it wasn't harmless but the framed Japanese erotica on Jedah Graf's walls was disturbing for in several of the drawings, in fact in the majority, the girls were very young.

On a wall beside Jedah's immense bed was a lascivious rendering of a girl of ten or eleven. The drawing was so particularized, you would think it must be based upon a photograph. The girl's black hair had been arranged geisha style, with glittering combs. Part-naked, in a kimono far too large for her, the girl primped and preened as if before a mirror. Drawn in swirls of black ink, the girl startled with a crimson rosebud mouth and two red nipples on her flat breasts.

A black-lacquered folding screen, with obscene likenesses of male and female genitalia amid flowers. Here and there a childish face peeping out.

On a bureau were glossy pornographic magazines and travel brochures advertising EXOTIC BANGKOK HOLIDAY—12-DAY "FREE AS THE WIND" JOURNEY FOR THE ADVENTURER OF THE EXOTIC. In one of the brochures were photographs of young girls in school uniforms, white socks; their black hair straight-cut in bangs falling to their eyebrows. Some of the girls had been luridly made up, some were not.

I pushed the brochures from me, I wasn't going to look further.

I felt a wave of dismay, disgust. Sex holidays! These were the trips abroad Jedah Graf took.

I was angry now. I began to open the bureau drawers.

Rummaged through my relative's expensive underwear, his socks. *You don't want to know* and yet I continued to look until at last, in the lowermost drawer, my fingers closed upon something cool, and plastic: a large black- and yellow-winged butterfly preserved in Plexiglas, about six inches in diameter.

Was this my butterfly, that Daddy had brought back to me from Thailand, years ago? The one I'd hoped to give away but was returned to me, after my mother wrote to the mothers of my friends? Or was the butterfly Jedah Graf's, similar to my own?

For years I'd kept the butterfly on a windowsill in my room. It was associated in my mind with shame: *Merilee, how could you!* Later, when I was in high school, it seemed to have disappeared. I'd thought maybe it had fallen behind my desk, or beneath my bed. I hadn't looked for it extensively. The poster with Lilac Jimson's picture on it also disappeared. I hadn't seemed to care, much. Once I'd become popular with boys, my life became complicated.

After the night I'd waited for him and was rudely rebuffed, Daddy became remote to me. It was difficult to believe that the man who could scarcely hide his boredom with his daughter could care that a tourist gift he'd brought her from Thailand, or even the pink pearl "heirloom" necklace, was missing.

Mom had been the one who'd cared. In her panic at arousing Daddy's wrath, she'd interfered with my giving of gifts to girls more deserving than I was.

Slowly I turned the Plexiglas butterfly in my fingers. The larger, upper wings appeared to be uniformly black, unless you looked closely and saw striations of black; the lower, smaller wings were exquisitely marked, symmetrical black lines, like ink, on a pale ethereal yellow. On the plastic surface were small scratches that looked familiar to me, but really, I could not know if this object had ever belonged to me.

Next, I pulled from the drawer a folded piece of stiff paper. Immediately I recognized the garish yellow poster, the urgent black letters as alarming now as they'd been in 1988:

MISSING 11-YR-OLD
LILAC JIMSON

Poor Lilac! The poster was badly creased, but Lilac's shining eyes and wide smile were unchanged.

But I couldn't determine if the poster was mine. So many posters with Lilac's face and name on them had been displayed in Mt. Olive, why would Jedah Graf have needed to take mine from my desk drawer?

Also in the bureau drawer were: a woman's mother-of-pearl hairbrush, with red-gold hairs (whose? no one I knew), a tarnished silver charm bracelet, a cosmetic kit with badly soiled powder puffs; a woman's sheer black stocking, with jagged runs. I held in my hand a German figurine of a plump, annoyingly apple-cheeked child, an exact match for figurines displayed in Aunt Cameron's house. And there was a sheet of stiff stationery crookedly folded, a desperate scrawled message in green ink:

Plaese no more—
I am so unhappy—
Will you call me—

A sign from you—
Dont hurt me furhter—

E.

E.? Edith? I'd seen very little of my mother's handwriting but this seemed to resemble it. Astonished, I reread the message several times.

I was upset now. I yanked the heavy drawer out so far that it fell to the floor, and something clattered at my feet: the sculpted-glass heart.

I snatched it up, staring in disbelief. Uncle Jedah had taken it! All along, he'd known exactly where it was.

I turned the glass heart in my fingers, to see that it hadn't been cracked. It was whole, unblemished: beautiful as I remembered, but it seemed slightly smaller.

I was squatting on the hardwood floor amid a pile of men's silk socks, pajamas, voluminous boxer shorts. I held the glass heart in my hand as my own heart pumped with adrenaline. I must have looked distraught, stunned. I could not have said where I was, my thoughts were so confused.

I'd heard no one approach. I had not heard the man's heavy footsteps on the stairs. Noiselessly, he'd appeared behind me. Almost gently he said: "Merilee."

In his shirtsleeves, frowning, there was Jedah in the doorway. That massive man, frowning. His face with its broad forehead and jaws was suffused with blood, of embarrassment or indignation. I scrambled to my feet, alert as a threatened animal. Thinking *He could strangle me. No one would know.*

I was furious. I wanted to scream at him. I held the glass heart in my fist, shaking it so that Jedah would know that I knew, now. "You stole this—didn't you! You—all along—you had it! Uncle Jedah how could you! You were laughing at me."

Jedah peered at the glass heart, and at the spillage of his clothes on the floor. Calmly he said, "Merilee, don't be ridiculous. You've behaved very rudely, to go through my things. I might ask, how dare *you!*"

"You stole from Daddy, and you stole from me. All along—"

"That isn't your father's glass heart, Merilee. If you'd looked more closely, you would see that it's smaller than the one you gave your father. Now give it here, and calm down."

"You're disgusting, a pervert! I hate you! I will never sell Daddy's house to you."

"Merilee, that glass heart is mine, I bought it in Venice a decade ago. If you check, you will see VENEZIA engraved in the glass."

This was preposterous. This was insufferable. As if I would believe such a lie. "Uncle Jedah, this is mine. Mine has VENEZIA engraved in the glass, too. How can you stand there pretending . . ."

I would have rushed past the man, but he blocked my way. I couldn't trust him not to touch me. I could see that he was speaking ironically, to mock me. Like an adult dealing with an emotional child, even extending his fat hand to me: "Give me the heart, Merilee. Before you break it in your hysteria."

I began to scream. I laughed. I shook my fist at the man.

"I'm not! Not hysterical! You—you're the thief!—liar!—pervert! I've seen the things in this room! The travel brochures! If Daddy had known about you! How disgusted Daddy would have been! I will never, never sell the house to you, not—"

Without warning Jedah strode forward. Another time I was startled by the agility of this corpulent man. His smile faded as he slapped my face, hard enough to send me staggering backward, and the glass heart flying from my hand.

I couldn't believe it. Uncle Jedah had slapped me. My right cheek throbbed with pain. Both my eyes leaked tears. I was crouching like a cornered animal, panting through my mouth. I had never been slapped before. I had never been mistreated before. Neither of my parents had even threatened to strike me. With a grunt of disgust Jedah stooped to pick up the glass heart, and examined it. His expression was one of hauteur, disdain. He would never apologize, he was angry with me still.

I might have escaped from the room at this moment except my legs were too weak to support me. My face was wet with tears, and burning.

"It's still in one piece. No thanks to *you*."

Jedah wiped the sculpted-glass heart on his shirtsleeve. He did no more than glance at me, as if the sight was repulsive to him. Sternly he said, "Go upstairs and put on your soiled clothes, that smell of your body. And take this cheap paperweight with you, since it seems to mean so much to you: it's yours."

He held the sculpted-glass heart out to me. I had no choice but to take it.

The Penitent

What is not recalled has not happened. Or, if it has happened, maybe it wasn't you to whom it happened but someone else.

After my mother died I had a friend who'd also lost someone in her family and we never spoke of our losses because there was nothing to say that wasn't maudlin, futile, or tinged with anger that made our jaws tremble. We were drinking friends. We were a matched pair: brunettes with smudged eyes and wanly pretty faces, sweet drunks and not belligerent drunks, girl-drunks who insisted upon buying their own drinks and who preferred dark, off-campus, "adult" bars to college hangouts and fraternity parties. We acquired a reputation, on campus and locally. For we were distinguished from our undergraduate classmates by the sobriety of our drinking which was meditative and not gluttonous, as a Catholic might say the beads of a rosary. We were not drawn to drinking for reasons of celebration/flirtation/carousing/sex but only to get drunk. We never drank quickly to speed up the process and so we were rarely sick to our stomachs, at least publicly. We preferred each other's company to the company of men, knowing that men, even "nice" ones, were not reliable drinking companions. We were novelties who didn't become noisy when we drank but ever more quiet. We were not gigglers but brooders. We were sometimes funny when we drank, but never witty. We were not sardonic. We were not even sarcastic. We were nineteen at first, and then we were twenty. We were not sisters but were sometimes mistaken for twins. We each had money—credit cards, cash. We drank together on weekends at first, then three nights a week, or four, or five. Eventually we drank together every night though not always (not inevitably!) through the entire evening and night, at least that wasn't our intention for we were also students, and were, or had once been, "serious" students. We could stop drinking whenever we wished, we believed. We remembered to eat nourishing food except when we forgot, or hadn't time. We preferred soft or liquefied foods to solids, which required effort to chew. We preferred booths, not bar stools; for you can fall from a bar stool, but rarely a booth. We preferred blues numbers on jukeboxes not pop rock. We preferred drinks with festive names, in festive colors— Orange Blossom, Bloody Mary, Tequilia Sunrise, Jamaican Sunset, Puerto Rican Sunburst, Tropicana Surprise, Cosmopolitan, Metropolitan, Apple Cream Jack Hammer, Sloe Gin Fizz, Jungle Juice, Desert Juice, Sidecar, Chocolat Noir. We avoided beers and ales for their embarrassing propensity to rush to our smallish bladders and cause us to sway, stagger, stumble in the uncertain direction of the women's room. We avoided hard, stark, masculine drinks in shot glasses. For a while my favorite drink was Absolut vodka with Cointreau and a splash of cranberry juice and my friend's favorite drink was a Galliano Wallbanger. Our laughter together was not jarring or hysterical to cause other patrons to glance in our direction, wincing or grinning; our laughter was likely to be silent, a matter of shaking and shivering with a facial expression meant to suggest mirth, not pain.

We were each other's most trusted friend, for the interim of our drinking. When, in the late winter of 1998, after several bad episodes, I quit drinking, we drifted apart without regret or a backward glance.

During the interim of our drinking, we shared the intimacy of forgetting which is the sweetest of all intimacies. We shared blank patches of amnesia like dirtied sailcloth. CeCi, unless it was me, or both of us, would wake on the floor of someone's room or in a lounge in the student center or in "off-campus" housing in unfamiliar surroundings. We might wake in rumpled beds, or in the smelly backseats of cars. Though we were girl-drinkers who hoped to avoid male companionship sometimes it happened mysteriously that we were in the company of men, that's to say men's bodies in comatose states like our own. Though sometimes (the most merciful times) we woke alone and lay in that suspended state between the sweetness of oblivion and the wracking throb of hangover for as long as our smallish bladders would allow. The corollary to *Where are my clothes?* was the practical admonition *What is not recalled has not happened. Or, if it has happened, maybe it wasn't to you.*

It began to be that way, in Mt. Olive.

Where inside my head my uncle Jedah Graf loomed immense as a thunderhead cloud being blown southward from Lake Ontario. When not fully awake I felt the powerful arms gripping me like coils. The rubbery resilence of thick warm flesh. On his skin that was so much ruddier and healthier than my own, a faint scaly glitter that was the glitter also of his eyes fixed upon me, inescapable.

Often I heard Jedah's voice, so matter-of-fact, so gently informative, I glanced around to see who'd spoken: *Merilee! I am the only one who cares for you.*

In late July, I moved from my cousin's house to an apartment in a wood frame house near the river. I moved from my cousin's comfortable house on Summit Boulevard hoping to move beyond the radar of my vigilant Graf relatives. Suddenly I was living on the third, top floor of a mold-colored clapboard house on a street named Bushover. A shabby slipping-down neighborhood delicately called "mixed" by realtors. It wasn't a neighborhood where I knew anyone or was likely to be known and it wasn't a neighborhood in which you'd expect the daughter of the late businessman/philanthropist Dennis Graf but it was a neighborhood to swallow me up, and hide me.

One afternoon I drove back to the house on Lincoln Avenue, that would be my inheritance. On the odometer of my car I noted that it was 2.3 miles from the house on Bushover Street, much of the distance uphill. This time I parked in the driveway. I went directly to my father's study, ignoring the intervening rooms. I examined the teakwood desk another time, I tried the locked drawers which were still shut up tight. I tried the lowermost drawer of the filing cabinet: locked. The closet door: locked.

I felt someone observing me, bemused. What a child you are, Merilee! What a fool.

I thought *Locks can be forced, I could hire a locksmith to open these.*

I never would, though. I would never bring a stranger into my father's study, to violate his things.

I had disposed of the bottle of Dalhousie's single-malt Scotch after I'd finished it. I'd washed the glass and replaced it on a shelf in the liquor cabinet. This time, I didn't go near the liquor cabinet for it was not a drinking day.

I was surprised to see *Images of God* on the leather sofa. I'd thought that I had reshelved it and quickly I reshelved it now.

I had no intention of looking at any other art-books of my father's. I had no wish to see what lay inside the elegant, over-sized covers.

For the first time since I'd returned to Mt. Olive, I descended into the basement where, even in the family room, the air smelled of mildew and drains. There had been a summer storm the night before, and some leakage in the basement. I made my way in the direction of the old cellar, where the smells of damp earth and something organic and rotted were stronger. I'd thought that I might look into the earthen-floored cellar, but I couldn't bring myself to push against the grimy wooden door for fear that, if I did, the door would be stopped by someone, or something, lying just inside.

I was waiting. Without knowing why, or for what.

A strange leaden passivity fell over me. As, those last months of college, when I'd stopped going to classes and slept through much of the day until it was time for my friend CeCi and I to go out . . . But now I had no friend. I hadn't even a lover. I had only my thoughts of Uncle Jedah to terrify and comfort. That man who'd slapped my face so hard, I was certain I'd heard it crack.

Ruefully touching my face that felt warm, feverish. In wonder examining it in a mirror.

Expecting to see the cracks, in white skin like porcelain. Yet there were none visible.

Comfort

"Merilee."

He laughed, though clearly he was still angry. I was a sulky adolescent if repentant.

In disgust he saw that I was pale and undernourished, he chided me for taking such poor care of myself, living now in a third-floor walkup in a ridiculous neighborhood, what was I thinking? *Was* I thinking? He brought me to his handsome brownstone at 8 Stuyvesant Square where a cassoulet awaited us in a warming oven, and we ate hungrily in his gleaming white kitchen as before. This time, after only a moment's hesitation, he allowed me to help him.

This time, he determined how much wine I was to drink with each course. "Not a drop more, Merilee! And not a drop less."

The wine was a light red beaujolais from a Mendocino, California, vineyard with which Uncle Jedah seemed to be associated, as an investor perhaps. The cassoulet was rich and dense and delicious with lamb, sausage and bacon and salt pork, white beans.

"Eat, eat! You look half-dead, not a pleasant sight."

My smallish mouth worked slowly. Uncle Jedah's large voracious mouth worked rapidly.

Sharp-eyed Jedah saw that I was having difficulty chewing the sausage, which he called *kielbasa*. He leaned over to cut the slices into smaller portions for me.

There was a light cucumber raita. For dessert, *crème brûlée*.

"You will eat every bit of it, Merilee. Use your tongue."

My tongue! I laughed, for Uncle Jedah had to be joking.

Not in Uncle Jedah's bedroom on the second floor (where I dreaded to be taken) but in a room on the first floor which also contained a television set, Uncle Jedah brought me to see a "special" video.

"Sit, Merilee. You need to be comforted."

The sofa was long, low, and curved. Its fabric was a stone-colored suede soft as the skin of an unborn creature. Uncle Jedah positioned me beside him, in the crook of his left arm. How massive the man was, as if the act of eating had plumped him up further, and suffused him with an air of well-being and generosity. I would have been anxious about the "special" video except I'd had two and a half glasses of wine with the remarkable meal. I would have been anxious about sitting in such intimacy with my eccentric uncle except Jedah's manner to me this evening had been unfailingly gentle, if slightly chiding. He had not been harsh with me, there could be no question of his wishing to hurt me. I had every reason to think that he'd forgiven me for whatever I had done, that had so angered him.

My long hours of sleep had left me forgetful. Amnesiac patches like that old, soiled sailcloth dragging across my brain. To sleep is to forget. To sleep heavily is to forgive.

Through the meal, which like a solemn ritual had required

more than an hour to consume, Uncle Jedah hadn't said a word about my selling the cobblestone house to him. He'd only just remarked casually that the "blue hydrangea" I'd planted in a front flower bed had died because no one had watered it.

My shock must have shown in my face for Uncle Jedah reached over to squeeze my hand, laughing: "You are never off Uncle Jedah's radar screen, dear. For your own protection."

The room we were in reminded me of my father's study except its furnishings were sleekly contemporary. Instead of an antique desk, Uncle Jedah had a glass-topped desk with a chrome base. But there was a liquor cabinet, and there was a filing cabinet. Similar built-in shelves lifted to the ceiling, filled with oversized books and art-objects—carvings, sculpted pieces—at which I didn't wish to look too closely for I had the idea that they were primitive, and stark.

"You have been pulled down into the grave with him, and I will pull you out."

I didn't hear this, exactly.

Uncle Jedah wielded the remote control in his right hand like a wand. I steeled myself as the video began. At first I could not make out what the images were. Then I saw: a mammoth speckled-black hog, that must have weighed five hundred pounds, with pale pink teats, lay on her side in a posture of lazy, luxuriant bliss. For a long moment, we saw only the hog. Then, in a corner of the screen, a small hairless creature appeared, crawling to the hog to begin blindly and greedily to nurse: not a piglet, but a scrawny puppy. The camera moved in close, showing the puppy nursing at an enormous pink teat. The hog's eyelids quivered in a trance of

sensual pleasure. I laughed, I was so surprised. Whatever I had expected, I had not expected this. "Captivating, Merilee, eh? Only
just relax, and observe. And be comforted, my dear. Your head on
my shoulder."

So sleepy! I did as Uncle Jedah instructed.

III

Uncle Jedah Up-Close

"Eventually, you will make the practical decision to deed over the property to me, dear. I think so."

Jedah Graf! My relative was far more eccentric than people knew, or could have guessed. I smiled to think how Daddy would not have approved if he'd known very much about the personal life of his "right-hand man."

For here was a man for whom life was to be devoured: chewed, savored, swallowed, and ingested.

A man for whom what wasn't of use (in the crudest nutritional terms) was to be excreted.

Traveling, such a man stayed in only the very best hotels— older hotels, usually, with a distinct historic aura. In these hotels he dined at the renowned restaurant, or, in off-hours, at the elegant gentlemen's bar, ordering appetizers from the rakish bar menu that was sometimes chalked on a small blackboard (platters of fried oysters and calamari, roast beef sandwiches on dark grainy bread, *salmon cru,* seared tuna, imported expensive cheeses). Such a man drank only the finest wines, the finest blended Scotch whiskeys, the finest cognacs, rums, brandies and liqueurs. Sometimes while savoring his drink, he might smoke a very special cigar. In the dimly lighted gentlemen's bar with its astonishing array of glittering bottles (their quantity magically doubled in a mirror running the length of the bar), he was invariably the largest and most imposing figure, princely in corpulence. He was politely genial with the bartender but not friendly. For Jedah could only be friendly with a social equal. In profile, his large face with its muscled cheeks looked both imperial and youthful; his ruddy flesh seemed to glitter as with a dusting of fine, near-invisible mica-chips; his thick black hair sprang back from his forehead in slightly dandyish wings. His eyes were his most striking feature: large, intelligent and alert, with lashes so defined as to appear artificially blackened. Their expression was often inscrutable, mysterious. *Make me happy, and I will be very nice to you.*

As a lover, such a man would not be the physically active party for to be physically active would seem to him to be servile. A prince is one who is served, not one who serves. This had nothing to do with Jedah's size, his bulk that had long prevented him from easily seeing his own thighs and genitalia, but only with his refined sense of himself. He'd been Dennis Graf's right-hand man for so long, he seemed to have absorbed my father's steely will and he seemed, so far as I could know, even more self-sufficient than my father had been. (For Daddy had married, after all; and had had a strong sense of family ties.) Such a man could not feel sexual pleasure, even sexual arousal, unless his will controlled the scene.

I imagined Jedah Graf in luxurious foreign hotels, quietly conferring with concierges, distributing American currency to appropriate parties. A discreet tap at the American gentleman's door and a very young, very pretty girl-child arrives like a fresh bouquet.

And the large meaty hand reaches out to gather in the bouquet, in silence.

I was an antic little girl eager to make my uncle Jedah laugh.

Especially the kind of laughter that takes a worldly man by surprise.

Shaking out the beige apron I discovered in a drawer in his kitchen, and trying to tie it around my waist though the apron was voluminous as a tent on me. I felt like a child playing dress-up. I drew my fingers across red stitching on the front of the apron as if reading the odd, enigmatic aphorism like braille. EATING IS TOUCH CARRIED TO THE BITTER END

Jedah saw, and laughed. I was becoming more "lustrous"— "luscious"—every day, he said.

". . . hated my piano lessons know why?—because I tried, I tried so hard, tried not to make mistakes but the more anxious I was the more mistakes I made because I hadn't any talent for the piano, I was a good-girl pupil at the piano as in school but I had no talent, really. Why Daddy insisted that I take lessons for so many years I never understood. Almost never he'd listen to me play. He wasn't home in the evening and if he was, and if he asked me to play for him, he'd stand behind me at the piano reading the music over my shoulder which made me very nervous because if I made a mistake, if I hesitated, I could feel him about to interrupt me even if he didn't interrupt . . . This day, a Saturday in June, he dropped me off at my piano teacher's house on Onigara

Street but Mrs. Deiter wasn't feeling well so my lesson was cancelled. I decided not to wait for Daddy to return to pick me up but to start walking home. It was only about two miles. They didn't like me to walk on the road by myself, after Lilac Jimson girls were warned not to but sometimes I did anyway, we all did and no one knew. And I was sixteen now, and not a child. I liked it that Mrs. Deiter was sick, I hoped she'd be sick for my next-week's lesson, too. I'd walked about halfway home, I was climbing the Center Street hill, where it's parkland to one side, and I'd been watching for Daddy's car which I kept expecting to see. And there came a shiny black car like Daddy's, and there was a man behind the windshield but I wasn't sure if it was Daddy, I lifted my hand uncertainly, like this I lifted my hand, and it was so strange!—in the instant I lifted my hand the shiny black car seemed to swerve as in a gust of wind, passing by me and braking, I turned to see the car pull over at the side of the road, and I was panicked now that the driver wasn't Daddy, a man was opening his car door and leaning over but it wasn't Daddy, it was a man in dark glasses I didn't know, I'd attracted the attention of a stranger which was what I'd been warned never to do, since Lilac we'd all been warned, and now this man was halfway out of his car peering back at me, I thought he might be smiling at me, I wanted to laugh at him, I wanted to shout *You can't catch me!*, I was scared and excited, I wondered who he was, if he was the father of someone I knew, and I was about to run into the park when suddenly I saw that the man was Daddy after all . . . Daddy hadn't seemed to recognize me, either. He hadn't expected to see me walking home, climbing Center Street. I'd been just a girl to him, any girl, a girl in a shirt and jeans, and in the instant before he recognized me and I recognized him a certain kind of—a kind of look had passed between us, I think."

My voice faltered and went silent. I was breathing quickly as if I'd been hiking up the Center Street hill. Laughing in a paroxysm of fright *You can't catch me* running into the woods. Uncle Jedah nudged me to be quiet. It was a way he had of poking my arm, or my rib cage, or my breast, to settle me down if I became over-excited. A nudge that registered somewhere between a tickle and pain. He'd replenished my drink which was cherry-colored, yet not so sweet as you'd imagine.

"Continue."

"Oh, Daddy was so angry with me. Daddy's face all flushed and angry and I was afraid of him, for days he wouldn't forgive me, wouldn't look at me and I . . . I never knew why."

"No, Merilee. Continue what you were telling me."

I steeled myself for another of Jedah's nudges, this time harder.

I was anxious, upset. My bare toes curled and twitched. I couldn't remember a thing of what had happened that day except I never returned to Mrs. Deiter's house and never had to practice piano again. Whatever had happened was gone like gusts of wind blowing debris up into the air and scattering it. " 'Continue'—how? Uncle Jedah, I don't know how."

Uncle Jedah regarded me with mirthful eyes. He smiled slowly.

The blunt-edged silver ring from Mexico, on Jedah's thick fore-finger, was wedged against the base of my throat like a branding iron. When the pressure increased, I couldn't breathe and began to gag; when the pressure eased, I was able to breathe.

"But you do, Merilee. You know how."

He took me somewhere. An access road into the park. His face was severe as something carved. Take down your jeans, he said. Your panties. I began to cry. I fumbled with my clothes. He lost patience and began to strike me on the buttocks with the flat of his hand. Somehow, I was bent over a picnic table. The table was scarred with initials. The rubbery soles of my sneakers slipped in the damp grass. This might have been then, or later. It might have been that day or another day. I'd stopped crying. Or maybe I hadn't begun yet. Or it was night, I was in bed in the dark beneath the covers daring to touch my buttocks where the skin felt scalding-hot and had risen in welts that overlapped and crossed one another as in a complex braid I could not see but had to imagine.

Drifting into sleep and his fleshy face began to lose its shape like melting lard. His breath began to slow and to deepen *huhh huhh huhh* with a wet click beneath that might turn into a snore, or a sudden snort. His mouth slackened, saliva glistened on his lower lip. I lifted the sculpted-glass heart to examine his face that was immediately magnified: the skin was rough-textured with lines, creases, fissures, and tiny pits. There were discolorations in the skin and areas that shone with an oily glisten. I wondered were these micro-organisms teeming with their own life. I was repelled, fascinated by what I saw. I had smuggled the sculpted-glass heart into Uncle Jedah's bedroom. I examined his jaws, where hair follicles sprouted like barbed wire. (Jedah had to shave twice daily, he said. For his beard was "relentless.") His nose that exuded an air of dignity seen from a short distance looked, through the magnifying glass of the heart, like a tumor or goiter, swollen, discolored, a tangle of broken capillaries beneath the surface of the skin. His lips were enormous seen through the glass, strangely striated, a sickly-soft skin like that of an earthworm. I dared to bring the glass to his left eye, that was partially shut, a crescent of yellowish eyeball visible beneath the lid. Jedah's long, feminine eyelashes looked like ugly spikes close-up and the skin bracketing his eye was slack and creased and ochre-colored like rotting fruit. What I could make out of the eye itself shone with the slimy opacity of an oyster or clam.

"Uncle Jedah?"

I was hunched over the sleeping man. His breath clicked wetly and paused and erupted into a snort like that of a startled animal but he didn't wake. I had learned that Uncle Jedah rarely slept for more than an hour at a time. Because of his bulk, he had difficulty breathing unless he lay in a semi-upright position, head and shoulders propped against a pillow, and this was awkward to maintain for very long since he also twitched and shuddered in his sleep.

Beneath the cover, Jedah was naked. Rolls of flesh, the fatty torso covered in patches of grizzled hairs, bunchy breasts as large as my own with nipples like cranberries. I was fascinated by the rubbery resiliency of the man's body, that reminded me of a thick fat snake. His genitals were small, given his size: limp and soft-skinned as wormy lips and of the hue of stale blood. The penis was a slug sprouting from the enormous hairy belly, the scrotum was a flabby pouch the size of a man's fist that thrummed and throbbed with the heat of a slightly higher temperature than the rest of Jedah's body. (Uncle Jedah claimed that a temperature beyond 98° F. was required to preserve his sperm. The secretion of Jedah's sperm, too, was "relentless.") All the parts of my uncle's body, I dared to examine through the sculpted-glass heart. I laughed, I was breathless and excited. What Uncle Jedah had given me to drink (Devil's Kisses, delicious 160-proof vodka) lapped and flamed at the edge of my consciousness like a powerful surf breaking onshore, noisy, blinding, lethal if you misstep and fall. I was excited yet becoming exhausted. I had planned to slip away from my uncle's house and return to my own but the downstairs was darkened at 8 Stuyvesant Place and already I was feeling lonely. *He is the only one. The one who cares. Who knows me, and forgives me.* I hid the sculpted-glass heart beneath one of the smaller pillows on Jedah's enormous bed.

After this, my memory isn't clear. Nudging against the massive sleeping man whose breath came now slow and deep *huhh huhh huhh* so that I believed he would continue to sleep for a while, and I might press against him, the swelling bulk of him, the heat of him, the solace of Uncle Jedah who shifted to make room for me, with a fretful murmur. The crook of a heavy arm, the curve of fat flushed jowls I might press my own heated face against, gently. Or better yet bury my face in his neck, the fatty folds of his neck. Waiting for the oblivion of sleep.

Star

███████

"M er-i-*lee.*"

Up two steep flights of stairs in the clapboard house on Bushover Street my middle-aged cousin Beverly came to appeal to me, panting. Beverly smiled graciously like all the Grafs but her eyes registered alarm and hurt.

". . . we need to see more of you! We are all missing you, and worried about you. 'Merilee seems to be in a state of shock'— that's what people say. You don't return calls, you have been 'shunning' your own relatives. Your friends from high school have called *me*. Why, someone was even saying . . ." Beverly paused, glancing worriedly about the jumbled room that had the slovenly look of one of those dreams hastily assembled and inadequately imagined, a mere backdrop for existence, ". . . you are spending time in the evenings with Jedah Graf? You've been at Jedah Graf's house . . ."

Beverly's voice lurched, as if the prospect of my spending time with Jedah Graf *at his house* was too alarming to be uttered.

I had asked Beverly please to sit down, in an overstuffed shabby chair, but I was too restless to sit, leaning instead against the arm of another chair, or a sofa, my feet positioned bare and flat on the floor like one about to run. I knew that my hair hung in my face and my skin shone oily and sallow but I was trying to be gracious to my visitor, making a gift of my good-girl sweetness though willing the woman please to leave me alone.

I'd used up much of my energy for this new day simply by dragging myself out of bed and washing my face in rust-flecked water. The inside of my mouth tasted like an old soiled sponge that's been left in the sun to dry.

"Merilee, are you all right? You're looking so . . ."

Beverly reached out to touch me. I shrank from the touch for Uncle Jedah would have to be told and he'd disapprove.

I said, "I think that I'm fine, Beverly. I just need to be alone for a while. You can tell Aunt Cameron, and the others. And thanks."

"I'm not convinced that you're 'fine.' You look feverish, and you're behaving strangely." Beverly knew of my history of drinking etcetera. I could see her wanting to ask what I'd been ingesting. Wanting to lean close to me, to smell my guilty breath.

"I've been behaving normally for me, Beverly. I don't feel comfortable with being judged."

"No one is 'judging' you, Merilee. But we are concerned about you."

"I know! I'm grateful for your concern. But I have business to discuss with Jedah Graf, you know he's the executor of my father's estate. I have to make a decision about the house. It's so much more complicated, death is so much more complicated than I would have thought, and Uncle Jedah . . ." I ceased speaking, close to saying *Uncle Jedah is all I have of Daddy now.*

Beverly was sympathetic. Beverly meant to comfort me. Yet somehow, we began arguing. Beverly seemed to be warning me against Jedah Graf and I said, hotly, that Jedah was the only person who cared about my father's estate, and about me. And Beverly flared up, the hurt in her eyes deepening to something like insult: "Merilee, that's simply not *true*. We all care about you except you keep us at arm's length, you always have. Your mother was the same way . . . Poor Edith!"

Poor Edith. I couldn't believe that Beverly would bring up this painful subject.

"If the family was concerned about 'poor Edith,' they certainly kept their feelings to themselves all those years. 'Poor Edith' could have used some friends in Mt. Olive."

"Merilee, that's ridiculous! Your mother shunned us, just as you are doing. We reached out to that woman, how many times my mother tried to befriend her, always it was—'Not now, I can't right now, sorry I can't talk right now, I don't feel well, goodbye'—Edith would hang up the phone in a panic. No one could make sense of your mother's behavior and after a while we all just gave up and who can blame us!"

"I don't want to talk about this, Beverly. I don't feel well either and I want to be alone."

Beverly frowned. Her aging-girlish face was flushed in indignation. "You're alone too much, and when you're not alone you're with *him*."

Beverly heaved herself out of the shabby plush chair. Though I'd been willing her to leave now that she was about to leave I felt a stab of regret. Uncle Jedah would insist upon knowing about this visit which he would label an intrusion, and he would want to know the degree of my participation in it. Beverly said, in a lowered voice, her face darkening with the thrilled shame of uttering such things, "Your so-called 'uncle'! We don't believe that man is even a Graf—he's of some other, alien stock—you can see it in his eyes. Why Uncle Dennis trusted him so, I can't imagine. Ask Jedah to tell you how he nearly got in very serious trouble a few years ago, but managed to squirm out of it. In Chautauqua Falls—or maybe it was Port Oriskany, where he has a place—he'd evidently drugged a young woman to 'paralyze' her—someone he'd picked up somewhere. The woman must have been bought off, or the police, because no charges were ever filed, and Dennis managed even to keep the news out of the papers. That's your precious 'Uncle Jedah.'"

I wasn't hearing this. I was pressing the palms of my sweaty hands against my ears. I told my gloating cousin that she had to leave now, I wanted to be alone.

Beverly leaned close, peering at me. The color was up in her cheeks. "That red mark on your throat, Merilee? As if something sharp was pressed into your skin, at the base of your throat? It has the shape of a star, Merilee. I wonder whose star it is?"

The Brace

. . . *a kind of metallic back brace, that extended to the neck and the back of the head. So that my spine, my neck, and my head were secured. And my arms were folded tight across my (naked, flattened) breasts in a pose like that on a funeral urn and secured by a metallic grid that locked into place. And my legs were spread wide to the point of excruciating pain, as if the thighs were about to be torn from their sockets; spread wide, exposing my (naked) belly, thighs, vagina.*

This was The Brace, as Uncle Jedah called it. His promise was that my ordeal would last only as long as I wished: not a moment longer, and not a moment less.

"God Forgive Me"

▬

In Port Oriskany on North River Street where my uncle Jedah owned property in a neighborhood of old brick row houses, derelict warehouses and small factories. Where, when the wind blew south-south-east, the air glowed with an undersea phosphorescence and smelled like toxic yeast. ". . . need to get high, see? I'm having a fucking time like this."

She stabbed angrily at the air with the edge of her little hand, in a horizontal arc. Meaning life on a horizontal level, life on a flat plane. She was laughing/frantic, glittery. Her mascara eyes shone. All her gestures were bird-like, stabbing. I stared at the piercings in her face that looked like silver stitches in her nose, eyebrows, lower lip. Her small feet in stiletto-heeled lizard boots to the knee, prancing about the room as in a dance on hot coals.

Uncle Jedah leaned forward, interested. His manner was polite, bemused. Here was a gentleman.

"And why, Monique, is that?"

"*Why? Why'd* I want to get high?" Monique grinned at Jedah, hands on her little hips. "*Why'd* anybody want to get high, that's a serious fucking question, mister?"

Jedah murmured what might be interpreted as an apology. Ever the gentleman.

"If I provide you with something to lift your spirits, Monique, you'll be a happy girl, eh? You'll be grateful."

"Ohhh hey: I'm grateful now, mister. You, taking me in like you did. I know I can trust you."

"And I can trust *you*."

A kind of glow or glare passed between them. Neither was looking in my direction. Yet the implication was, in my uncle's remark, he could trust Monique (whom he'd never met before tonight!) but maybe not me.

Uncle Jedah didn't mean this. I didn't think so. It was a game he was playing with our little friend. Maybe.

I'd been drinking since mid-afternoon. Vodka, and then tequila, now Bacardi Puerto Rican rum. My pulsebeat was erratic. I was inclined to be edgy, suspicious. I was concerned that my uncle had plans for a game involving Monique and excluding me.

Monique was very short: hardly five feet tall in her sharp stiletto heels. At a first glance she looked young—years younger than me—but I was beginning to see she might be older. Her mannerisms were those of an adolescent, her face was both childish and oddly wizened, like something carelessly crushed in a hand. Her lips were outlined in bright greasy red in the way a child might apply makeup, in innocent excess. Her small damp eyes were sooty with eye shadow and mascara and her eyebrows had been plucked to thin, arching lines. Her hair had been so bleached by chemicals it had no lustre, like straw. Her forehead was low, and lined.

She wore a purple suede fringed vest, bare breasts beneath, and a skin-tight black vinyl miniskirt exposing her mysteriously lumpy, pale thighs. Across the small of her back was the tattoo in black gothic letters: GOD FORGIVE ME.

Monique was drinking rum, and chattering continuously like a deranged bird. She punctuated her chatter with bursts of laughter angry-sounding as a zipper rapidly zipped/unzipped/zipped to no purpose.

In the scenario, "Monique" was my friend? My dear friend? We were meant to be affectionate with each other? Was that it? In the stage setting my uncle had provided us? (A room that resembled a motel room. Except, on the floor, where you'd expect to see a rug, was what appeared to be a plastic covering over something like a tarpaulin, laid on bare floorboards.) I had been reluctant to approach her, but Uncle Jedah had commanded me.

Now, on the palm of his large hand, two round yellow pills: "yellow jackets." For Monique.

Uncle Jedah winked at me. "Not you, dear. I think not."

It was late, and then it was later. There were few lights in the building (a partly furnished duplex) and the blinds on all the windows upstairs and downstairs were drawn. I'd had the impression when we'd arrived that the properties on both sides were vacant. Much of this end of North River Street appeared to be vacant. Monique danced to her own high-pitched singing, drank rum and popped yellow jackets and clattered about the room excited by the rich gentleman's interest in her. He was so formal in his speech, so clearly admiring! And Monique was so trusting, as if she'd played this game, or one very like it, many times before.

For such a small person, weighing perhaps eighty-nine pounds, she seemed to take up a lot of space. Bumping into me, stabbing me with her stiletto heels and giggling: "Sor-*ry*."

This duplex in a run-down brick row house in Port Oriskany was not a place I knew. It was sparely furnished with mismatched items. It had the look and smell of a place in which no one lived. Its walls were bare and unadorned unlike the walls of Uncle Jedah's brownstone in Mt. Olive. All the furniture was made of synthetic "wood" and vinyl that should have been easy to keep clean, yet appeared to be grimy. On the floor beside the bed, leaning against the wall, was a cracked mirror framed in oddly ornate beveled glass, that reminded me of a similar mirror in the cobblestone house, hanging on the wall in a first-floor room my mother had referred to vaguely as the cloakroom. (As if "cloak" was a term that would have been known to her.) If we'd been alone, without perky little Monique, I would have asked Uncle Jedah about the mirror.

But, without Monique, my uncle and I wouldn't have been here. I didn't think so.

As in a motel room, the bed dominated. A king-sized bed with a glazed-looking headboard of some slick, synthetic material meant to look like satin. When Uncle Jedah lowered his weight onto the edge of this bed, the springs creaked loudly. Monique giggled, as if the well-dressed corpulent gentleman with the avid eyes had farted.

"You're a big one, ohhh man. But see, I like 'em big. I like the kinda man, you can grab hold of and hang *on.*" Monique licked her greasy lips and made clawing/clutching gestures with her little hands.

Uncle Jedah laughed heartily. The bedsprings creaked louder. Clearly he was charmed by Monique with her glittery face-piercings and provocative tattoo.

Was I jealous seeing how my uncle watched Monique, seemed to be memorizing Monique, as weeks ago he'd watched me, well maybe yes. (It was September now. A dull-rainy night. What I'd glanced up naively to see as a full moon had been an ordinary streetlight as we'd turned the corner onto North River Street.) Did I dislike Monique, did I resent her, did I want something bad to happen to her, well maybe yes.

Uncle Jedah had assured me it was only a game. When I'd asked what kind of game he said that it was in the nature of games not to be serious and to have no lasting consequences. And that was all I needed to know.

When I asked what were the rules of the game, how would you know if you'd won (or lost) he'd laughed in a pleasant unperturbed way that indicated he was losing patience with me, and squeezed the nape of my neck with his strong fingers.

"Trust in Uncle Jedah, dear. You know that."

I knew. But I needed to be reminded.

Monique in her purple fringed vest, bare white breasts visible beneath, had been standing in the rain on a littered pavement outside a liquor store whose front windows were protected by iron grids. She'd looked very young from across the street, her movements awkward and antic and her small pug-face glittering with piercings like those goth-girls you might see at the mall, black lipstick, eye shadow and tongue-rings in their early teens. Uncle Jedah sighted her like a predator shark: "There. That one." I thought *No I will not* even as Uncle Jedah nudged me out of the car. *Fuck you Uncle Jedah I will not pick up a hooker for you* I thought even as I approached the hooker smiling, "Hi!" Monique stared at me blank-faced. For a moment a look of fear—a look, almost, of intelligence—sharpened her face. Those persons who might approach her at such a time and in such a place in a lightly falling September rain were nothing like me and so Monique suspected a trick. "Hey: you a cop?" she asked, and I said, "Do I look like a cop?" feeling my face suffuse with blood, that this bizarrely costumed and made-up little woman teetering in stiletto-heeled lizard boots should be peering so closely at me, that my life after Daddy's death should have brought me to this extreme. "My uncle is the one who wants to meet you. Over there." Monique squinted past me across the street at the idling Porsche, where Uncle Jedah sat behind the wheel watching us. Seeing him, seeing the showy car, Monique grinned and waved. This was more like it: a man.

On North River Street, as the hour passed into night and rain pelted against the windows, Monique became ever more feverish, excited. She drank rum in large reckless swallows. Her skin looked flammable. I wondered what the combination of alcohol and methamphetamine did to the human brain. The tiny silver wires—rings, clamps—in her face gleamed like metallic stitches. Uncle Jedah had examined Monique's several tattoos and listened with interest to Monique's stories of how she'd acquired them. "'God Forgive Me'—it's the oldest tattoo, I got it when I was just a kid. See, it's kind of fading now, I sweat so much here." Monique was caressing the small of her back, thoughtfully. "Only way I can see it is in a mirror, the words backward."

It seemed clear, not part of a game, that Uncle Jedah—"Mr. J." to Monique—was fascinated by her. "Merry"—as Uncle Jedah had identified me, to Monique—was trying not to be visibly jealous telling herself that Uncle Jedah would not be bringing Monique with him back to Mt. Olive, he would be bringing *her.*

Part of the time, Uncle Jedah seemed to be interviewing Monique. Asking her which creature she'd choose to be: a lioness, a dolphin, an elephant, an egret. I drifted from the room carrying my drink and when I returned there was Monique sitting close beside Mr. J. with one of her lumpy white-skinned legs slung over his fat knees. In the effort to think hard and to impress him, Monique was perspiring. Her manner was both coquettish and anxious. ". . . like if I was a lioness, I'd be a beautiful animal and very strong and could run fast but I'd have to hunt for food every day, it would be living food I would have to kill and devour raw, and that would, like, disgust me, and when I got old and slow, how'd I hunt? Say my foot—my paw—gets infected, how'd I run? So maybe I should say a dolphin, that's one of those seal-type things in the ocean?—not a fish but an animal, like?—but if I was a dolphin I'd get trapped in one of those big fishermen's nets, that are two miles long in the ocean?—isn't that what happens to dolphins? I could say elephant, 'cause an elephant is sure big, but if I was a wild elephant like in Africa I'd be hunted for my ivory tusks, I could attack my enemies if I could get close enough to them and stomp them to death but if it was human hunters they could shoot me before I got that close, and size wouldn't matter a damn. But if I was an e-grit—you say that's a 'beautiful white shore bird'—I could fly away, far from any human beings. I could find some place in the northern woods. See, I hate people. I mean, I don't hate all people, there's exceptions, but mostly people are evil and want to hurt you, so if I was a bird I'd fly away to where there weren't any people, that way I could survive." Monique broke off with a burst of high-pitched laughter.

Uncle Jedah stroked the lumpy white-skinned leg slung so clumsily onto his fat knees. "An egret is an excellent choice, Monique. An expression of the spirit. I can envision you as purely spirit, flying into the northern lights. A creature of beauty, straining to escape the anguish of existence."

Monique squirmed with pleasure, being so praised. She cast her sooty eyes in my direction wondering at my silence.

"Mr. J." had engaged Monique's services for the night, for a flat fee of five hundred dollars. It was natural for Monique to wonder what the role of "Merry" would be, in this arrangement.

Every glance Monique directed at me, I avoided. My face was brittle as glass. Alcohol coursed in my veins like a richer, more dependable blood. But I was trembling, a terrible rage seemed to be building in me.

Uncle Jedah said, with a chiding glance at me, "Merry is in a sulk, I'm afraid. Usually she isn't so socially maladroit. But she has suffered a loss, that seems to her tragic. And the sorrow of her loss," Uncle Jedah continued, ominously, with the air of one choosing each of his words carefully, "is that she doesn't know its magnitude. Yet."

"Ohhh hey: what kind of loss?" Monique crinkled her pug-face at me in immediate, exaggerated sympathy.

"Merry doesn't wish to discuss it with a stranger, I'm sure."

"I don't want to be a stranger! I want to be one of you, like a family."

Uncle Jedah laughed. I'd turned away disgusted. Thinking

Why am I here? I can leave any time. I had a vision of myself running along North River Street in the rain.

Uncle Jedah in his mode of gentlemanly interrogator was asking Monique about her own family, which elicited lengthy, rambling, drunken responses. Monique had been kicked out of her home as a young girl, she claimed. She'd run away with a man. She'd been in trouble with the law. She'd been incarcerated in the Port Oriskany Women's House of Detention without any trial, for four months. ". . . I had a little baby, last year. But it was too little, y'know? Way too little." With her twitchy hands Monique shaped a baby the size of a small cat. "It could not live." She paused, her lower lip trembling. She had the look of a child who has recklessly stepped into a ditch mistaking it for a shallow puddle, who has begun to realize her mistake. "See, it wasn't my fault! The bastards arrested me, and brought me to the station, and had the baby they'd found in the, in some place I didn't know, how it got there I don't know, like in a Dumpster, but I didn't put it there, and they did some tests, or pretended they did, all the while I was incarcerated, I was strung out and sick and didn't care if I lived or died, anyway they did these tests, a lawyer came to tell me, from Legal Aid, the water in the lungs—it showed my baby was dead before . . ." Monique spoke rapidly and excitedly, glancing from Uncle Jedah's face to mine, and back again, eager to hold our interest. How like a mysteriously deformed child she was, with her wizened little face and twitchy body! I stared at her, repelled by her. I could not believe the things she was speaking of in a bright chattery way like a TV weathergirl. GOD FORGIVE ME gleamed with sweat across the small of her back.

Monique began to complain in a whining voice, she was

coming down from her high, "Mr. J." needed to supply her with something more, fast. Uncle Jedah reached for the valise he'd placed between his feet. He took out a silver cigarette case, and handed Monique a cigarette. "You'll like this, dear."

I saw then that Uncle Jedah was wearing gloves. Thin, translucent rubber gloves. I went away to another part of the duplex. I found a bathroom, a stained sink and toilet bowl in a closet-sized room. One of the faucets emitted a thin trickle of brackish water. I heard Monique's squealing laughter and Uncle Jedah's deeper voice beneath. I thought *He is going to hurt her.* Then I thought, more calmly *He would not hurt her, not with me as a witness.*

At the rear of the duplex was a cluttered storage room and to get to the door beyond I had to climb, and crawl. Somehow it had happened, I was barefoot. I couldn't remember what I had done with my shoes. The door was locked, and I could not force it without making noise. I managed to open a window, that was covered in grime. Beyond the window was an alley, and beyond the alley what must have been North River Street, deserted at this hour. Still rain was falling. The air was suffused with a yeasty sulphurous smell like baking bread gone wrong. The nighttime sky was opaque, reflected with odd patches of red-tinged light. It had a festive look, a look to assure *Not much is real, and even if real, it won't last long.* Steel mills, factories on the west side. I'd climbed onto the windowsill, wincing with pain. I was panting, desperate. In my desperation I'd become sober. The window was no more than two feet square but I managed to force myself through it. My body was contorted as a monkey's. As Monique might have done, or Lilac my friend. I fell to the pavement, trying to brace my fall with my hands. I could hear them back inside the room. But they had nothing to do with me. A female cry high-pitched as a squeaking bat. A dissolve of laughter.

I was crawling behind trash cans. I'd turned my left ankle in my fall. I wanted to scream but had no voice. The screams behind me were short, like gunshots. I crawled somewhere to hide. Then my bladder burst, and afterward I had to crawl to another place to hide. I thought *The rain will wash away my urine, there will be no way of identifying me.* I was hugging my knees against my chest. When Uncle Jedah found me, the rain had stopped. I felt a foot prodding me. My uncle was too corpulent to bend over me, even if he had wished to bend over me. I saw that his face, that I'd imagined would be suffused with wrath and disgust at my behavior, was calm, as if purged of all passion. Quietly he said, "Get up, Dear. Come with me. It's over."

911 Call Not Made
9/8/04

I *want to report. I think a crime was committed. I think I was a witness.*
I did not actually see a crime but I think a crime was committed. I did not
see the consequences of any crime. I was not an actual witness to any
crime.

I want to report, I did not see. I heard, but I am not certain what
I heard. I am a good person, in my heart. I know that I am a good per-
son. I will lift the phone receiver, I will plead that I am a good person. I
will plead, Help me!

Two Ghosts

He thanked me for the gifts I'd mailed to his little niece Buena: "First time in her life she'd ever gotten anything in the mail with her name on it, for sure she's gonna remember you all her life."

Maybe there was an edge to his voice. Maybe he was eyeing me suspiciously. Or maybe with interest.

Carefully I said, "Well. Buena is a beautiful child."

As if that would explain my eccentric behavior.

Jimson and I were having drinks in Judge's Bar & Grill on the south edge of Mt. Olive. We were uneasy, excited in each other's company. We hadn't spoken since Jimson visited my father in the hospital on the eve of my father's death.

My voice had caught a little on "beautiful." Pain must have shown in my face. It came to me in a rush of feeling, how I wanted a child of my own. Like Buena, like Lilac. I wanted a child with this man. There was a hole in my heart that had to be filled, or I would die.

Talking of his niece, and how her "motherfucker daddy" hadn't wanted her to be born, Jimson spoke passionately. He leaned his elbows on the scarred tabletop. His head was close-shaven and his jaws were covered in a mean stubble. Judge's was a country tavern and no place I knew but Jimson seemed

comfortable here. The funky jukebox played Johnny Cash and
not hip-hop but among the majority of mostly white men there
were some dark-skinned patrons. A mixed-race couple wouldn't
be stared at.

Jimson was drinking beer, from the bottle. I was drinking
ginger ale. He'd laughed at me. Wanting me to know he knew
full well what a drunk I was in my pretty-white-girl secret heart.

If anyone knew me, Roosevelt Jimson did. You'd have thought
we'd been lovers years ago. Far back as high school. Maybe someday, if things worked out between us, we'd come to think that
had been so, ourselves.

I'd moved to Bushover Street having reason to believe that
Selena Jimson had friends in the neighborhood and one day
we'd meet by chance in the street and afterward Selena would
mention to her brother Roosevelt that she'd met me, and where
I was living, and Jimson would show up at my door. And so it happened, just that way.

I couldn't invite Jimson into my apartment, I wasn't ready for
that intimacy. Instead, we drove out to Judge's Bar & Grill where
it looked like Jimson's intention was to get drunk.

Leaning his elbows on the tabletop between us. Speaking vehemently, of Buena, and of Lilac. He was wearing a dark flannel
shirt and work trousers. His shirt sleeves were rolled up past his
elbows. There were small scars, near-invisible pits and abrasions
in his singed-looking skin. His eyes were heavy-lidded, and the
whites had a tarnished luster. As always in the man's close prox-
imity I began to feel unsettled, unbalanced. Wanting to clutch at
something, to keep my balance. Saying words I'd prepared,
though it wasn't the right time, but my words were a gift I'd

wrapped and had now to give, no matter with what a blank staring look it was received: "I know that I remind you of Lilac, and when you see me, you think of Lilac. I know that, Jimson. But I think that could change."

Jimson did give me a blank staring look. But only briefly. Then he looked away, trying not to be embarrassed.

"Fuck, honey: things change by themselves, or don't. Not a hell of a lot we can do about it."

He was some "damn dumb ghost" stuck in the same place, he said. Going over and over the same "fuckin'" ground. Sixteen years after Lilac disappeared he still woke up crazy and sweating thinking there's this place Lilac might be, in the gorge, or along the river bank, that nobody thought to look, and he's desperate to get there. "See, nobody wants to live with a ghost, like me. Nobody wants to employ a ghost, like in law enforcement. What's hard is that Lilac was never found. We say 'Lilac was never found' not 'Lilac's body was never found.' Because, in the family, you never think that way when somebody is missing. As a rookie cop, I was sensitive to that. I was sensitive to vocabulary. I know what it is, when a homicide isn't closed. When a body isn't found. For a long time, people avoided us, especially my mother. They'd cross the street not to have to talk to us. Cops hassled my father, he'd get drunk and obstreperous. It was a good thing, he left us. There wasn't any good coming out of him staying with us. My sisters and me, we came to accept it. I know, Lilac is gone. Dead."

Jimson paused, stricken by his own words.

I leaned over to touch his hand on the table. A tight-closed fist, with big scarred knuckles.

"Why I fucked up on the force, is I can't get my head out of that time. I went into police work because of Lilac. I'd gotten to know some cops on the Mt. Olive force, and I liked them. And they liked me. Still, I was a fuck-up in high school. I was doing drugs, and trying to get into dealing, and one night some guys beat the shit out of me, older guys from Rochester, and it turned out good they did because I'd of gotten deeper into it if they hadn't, by now I'd be long dead. I got in trouble at school, was suspended a few times then expelled. Any job I'd get, I'd fuck up and get fired. People who liked me, or tried to like me, got afraid of me. I was like something flammable, the least spark sets off. It was bad enough my mother losing Lilac, I gave her grief, too. Then one day, out of nowhere Momma said, 'Mr. Graf wants to talk with you.' She'd used to work for him. When I was in high school. I didn't know much about your family, but I knew that there was some 'sickness' to do with your mother, Momma said. Why Momma stopped working for your family, I don't know. She wouldn't say. It never made much of an impression on me. I'd hardly know where my mother worked, except it was 'white folks on the Ridge.' That's where all the 'housework' was, in those big houses. Or lawn work, or 'handyman.' I was about eighteen when Momma told me about 'Mr. Graf,' I went to see him in his office, and he asked me what was I doing with my life, did I know how I was hurting my mother, and I was ashamed, and said yeah I guess I knew, and your father says, 'So what are you going to do about it, Roosevelt?' and I said I didn't know, maybe go back to school, and he told me that was right, that's what he hoped I would say, because I was a 'damned smart kid'—'too smart for your own good, sometimes.' So we worked it out, I would get my high school diploma in the night school, and days I would work at this place he'd got me a job at—crating things, loading trucks for Graf Imports, Inc. He says to me then, he'd pay my tuition at any college I could get into, like the community college, or the tech school, and I said I wanted to go to the police academy, and your father looked at me like at first he thought it must've been a joke, but I was serious, and he said, 'All right, Roosevelt, I can help you there. It's a deal.' And we shook hands."

He'd liked the academy, really well. He'd liked his teachers. He'd liked most of the other students. Trained to be a law enforcement officer you're trained in knowing your rank, where you stand, who you take orders from, it was like being a soldier in an army except you had your own life off-duty, and there wasn't any actual war. You might get killed, but the odds were 'way against it. Most cops, they'd never fired their guns. A lot of cops in a small town like Mt. Olive, they'd never even drawn their guns on duty. But they were trained, and the training was good: "You learn to act fast. Really fast. Not needing to think, but to 'react.' It places you in a position with the world, your senses are sharp and alert like you're a radar screen, you pick up signals civilians would never. You see, things civilians would never."

I asked Jimson what, for instance?

"In here? Now? I'm seeing where the exits are. It's automatic, I come into a place, I see the entrances, exits, including windows. I see who's in view, and if their hands are in view. The bartender, I been tracking him. Not for any reason, just he's a guy I know, I been watching him at the bar, talking with you here, I'm not really trying to record anything but it's like a tape is playing in my head, a surveillance tape, so I could tell you, if I was asked, some of the guys he's been interacting with, and any one of them, there's a sign one of them's drinking too much, acting like he might be trouble—I'd remember him, his face. The ones I can see, I can remember. The ones who've looked over at us, at you. There's been some guys looking, I'm aware of them. Every one of them." Jimson smiled, liking my surprised expression. "You think I'm not aware, Merilee? Of you, in here with me, how it affects some white guy? And you not noticing, I guess. Like it's all passing beyond you."

Now I glanced around, nervously. I wasn't sure that I saw anyone watching. Maybe I wasn't seeing clearly: my vision seemed blurred, blotched. Staring at Monique the other night I'd felt my eyes fill with tears until I wasn't seeing her, only just the outline of her, wavering like something underwater.

Jimson said it was all right, civilians never noticed much. The world passes beyond them and only when it hits them do they notice, and then, most of the time, it's too late.

"A civilian makes a poor witness. Even of something that happens to them personally. Like, you're hit by a runaway truck, you're the one who doesn't see the truck."

I told Jimson yes. I thought that must be so.

I said, "But a witness has to try, doesn't she. A witness can't shut her eyes and be blind."

If Jimson saw the tight look in my face, saying this, he didn't give a sign. There was in this man a wish not-to-see and not-to-witness I would have to respect.

Jimson told me how, a rookie on the Mt. Olive PD, he'd had access to computer files and could track down sex offenders more or less on his own. He wasn't a detective and had no business going into files but he'd taken down information, on days off he'd drive over to Port Oriskany, Buffalo, Niagara Falls, as far away as Albany, Yonkers, even Scranton, Pennsylvania where he'd gone to investigate an ex-con baby-raper who'd formerly lived in Port Oriskany. Because there'd been other girls Lilac's age and older who'd been abducted and never found, or raped and murdered and their bodies dumped in places like Highlands Park, and no perpetrator ever found. Going back to the late 1970s and into the late 1990s. There'd been five in all, possibly six or seven if you counted suspicious "runaways." Of course it wasn't clear that the same perpetrator was responsible. And some of it happened so long ago, DNA samples hadn't been taken. And by now even if the girls' bodies were exhumed, the DNA would be gone. "So I was getting a little crazy. Once you get into the computer, there's no limit. I could see where this was taking me, but I couldn't control it always thinking one more, one more name to track down, one more baby-raper to look up, if he's still alive. I talked to a lot of these guys over a period of just a year but only one reported me, and my lieutenant gave me hell. Over all, I was doing a good enough job. My superiors liked me O.K. There's not what you'd call an excess of blacks in Chautauqua County law enforcement so I was one black boy people could agree they liked, I hadn't done bad at the academy and I could relate to civilians and execute orders, if it was the right orders from the right officer. I got along with my partner, Italian guy in his forties, he liked me, liked to tease me, called me 'Roose.' Nobody ever called me 'Roose' before, it kind of stuck. The first-year reports on me were good. Except for the complaint from the baby-raper fucker in Scranton, claiming I'd been 'threatening' to him asking questions he didn't legally have to answer, my lieutenant liked me . . . Then one day last year my partner and I get this call, we're sent out to bring in some sick motherfucker who'd hurt a little girl. Lucky for me when we track down this son of a bitch he's black not white, he runs out of the back of the place he's staying in over on Mission Road, and I'm waiting. He had to be subdued, and I subdued him. He was resisting arrest, and I had to use force. Good thing my partner was present, I'd have killed the fucker. I'd have broke his face. I'd have broke his neck, his back. I was messing him up pretty good. I used my baton, also I used my fists and feet. Until they stopped me, it felt good." Jimson paused, smiling a mean smile. He was rubbing the knuckles of one hand with a look of satisfaction. "Lucky the fucker didn't die. Lucky for me, I mean."

I said, "Lucky for your family, too. People who love you. Maybe you need to think of them, not only of Lilac."

I'd begun to be aware of people watching us, in the corner of my eye. I was hoping there were no customers in Judge's, male or female, who might know me from high school. When we'd come into the tavern, Jimson had been greeted by a few people including the bartender but he hadn't introduced me. I wondered if any of these men were friends of Jimson's. If there were individuals here who knew Roosevelt Jimson, and weren't his friends.

"What I got to think of, honey, is present time: what am I gonna do for work."

"You're working for Wal-Mart, Selena said."

"Fuck I'm working for Wal-Mart! Not since last Saturday."

He'd had a disagreement with his supervisor, Jimson said. But he'd been ready to quit anyway. Now he was between jobs. Thinking of moving away. Except he was helping support Selena and Buena and some others. And he hadn't cleared up things here, yet.

I said, "You could return to police work, Jimson. It isn't forever, is it?—what happened last year?"

I would take this man's side. I would say *what happened*—not *what you caused to happen.* This fact passed between us, in a heartbeat.

Jimson drank, to avoid answering my question. The subject of the Mt. Olive Police Department was painful to him. I thought it must be Jimson's pride that had been injured. If he'd been suspended from the force. But I knew better than to press him.

He asked me what was my life now and I said I wasn't sure that I had a life, just now. This was too enigmatic for him. He wasn't even going to hear it. A mean look came into his eye. He meant to twist the knife a little, teasing: "Heard you're an 'heiress,' honey. Only 'heiress' I ever met. You'll be leaving Mt. Olive, right? Rich girl like you, there's not enough for you here."

I said, "There's everything for me here."

This remark too Jimson wasn't about to acknowledge. Without a word of explanation he shoved out of the booth to use the men's room, or anyway that's where I assumed he went unless he'd gone home and abandoned me here, which I didn't believe Jimson would do, in his heart he was too much the gentleman. Then I saw him at the bar getting more drinks. Bringing two icy bottles of beer back to us. One of these he pushed at me.

"Come off it, baby. This is your old friend 'Roos'velt.' "

Since North River Street, Port Oriskany, I hadn't had a drink.

Today wasn't a drinking day, I'd vowed. With a guy like Jimson, the temptation is to drink too much.

But somehow I was drinking. Telling myself it was only just beer. And soon we were laughing, and getting along fine. Our serious subjects were done for the night. Our serious subjects had made us anxious and were done for the night. A few swallows of cold beer in the right company, in the right place, and life is fine. Like you'd been driving with your brakes on. And now you've eased the brakes up. On a hill, going down. The thrill of feeling yourself gaining speed. Momentum. You think *This is the direction to happiness, at least.*

Special Delivery

Next day, at 11 A.M. of September 17, the mailman brought a special delivery packet for me from Jedah Graf. My first impulse was not to sign for it. Then I thought *I don't have to open this! I have the freedom to destroy this.*

Since the night in Port Oriskany, I hadn't seen Uncle Jedah. I hadn't spoken with him. I was terrified of him and could not return his calls on my answering machine, that were curt, bemused, subtly threatening. These messages I erased without listening to fully.

Inside the manila envelope there was no explanatory note from Uncle Jedah. There were two documents.

I thought *This is a mistake. I should not be reading this.*

The first sheet of paper I unfolded was a photocopy of a report from the CHAUTAUQUA COUNTY MEDICAL EXAMINER dated 5/25/97. The subject of the report was EDITH ANN GRAF, 51 (DECEASED).

My hands were trembling badly. I had difficulty reading the report. Columns of print, highly technical medical/chemical terms. At the bottom, unmistakable, was CAUSE OF DEATH OVERDOSE MEPERIDINE/XANAX/PERCODEN.

"Overdose."

My mother had died of a drug overdose, not a stroke.

Maybe I'd known. Maybe I'd always known. Drinking with my old, lost friend CeCi, I'd known.

The second enclosure was a handwritten letter on stiff dusky-rose stationery embossed with the letter *E*. My mother's handwriting resembled that of a child or an ill person, wavering and slanted in a dark purple ink. My eyes filled with moisture as I read, it took me some minutes to comprehend what I was reading.

May 11 1997

To my daghter Merilee

    I am writting this to make you feel, there was nothing to be done. I ~~know~~ accept it that you did not loveme, I am not a mother to be loved. I did not expect it from you, or anyone.

    When you read this I will be gone. That is my hope.

    At first it was so, I had hope in my mariage to your father. I loved him so much it was wrong I think for we should love God more but I was weak and beleived what he told me until there was the revelation in my mariage to make a mockery of it.

    I was not a good mother but I tryed for the beginning untill it was too late to continue. I should not have come to this house, where I have not been wanted. It was a wrong decesion on my part, I was ignorant at the time tho' not young. I was weak to marry D.G., I beleived that I loved him he was like no man who had ever spoke to me. I would learn later he did not care for "grown women" & esepcally he did not wish for a "woman to speak her mind" he would always say. He was not so disgusted with me at the begining. Now I am an "ugly cow" in his eyes but at the begining he would say of me I was a "good woman". When I began to be sick I needed more medicine than the doctor would give me. When I took the medicine from ~~xxxxxxx~~ opened my hand & saw what I was hiding he said, Your life is your own & walked away from me in disgust.

Each time he was gone he would say to me, Your life is your own. Which would mean that I could distroy this life when I wished. When I would say, But what of our daghter he would be angry & not answer becase I beleive he would forget, there was a daghter in this house. When he would return from one of his trips he would be sad seeming then & would tell me he would not be gone any longer but later, he would change his mind. For a "grown woman" was repulsive to him & I think a dagther also was ~~xxxxx~~.

I am very tired now Merilee, I am sorry to say goodbye while you are gone to school but when you recieve this you will understand more. I tryed to love you I am sorry

Your mother Edith

It was a suicide note.
My mother had committed suicide.

Dying, even as she'd taken a fatal quantity of pills, she'd written to me. She had thought of me. Yet the letter had never been given to me, my father must have appropriated it. And, in time, my uncle Jedah.

I began to cry. As I hadn't been able to cry at my mother's funeral. Trying to remember the final time I'd spoken with her, but I could not. It must have been one of my quick careless calls from college, made out of guilt, in resentment. I tried to remember the final time we'd touched each other, and I could not.

I stood with my mother's letter in my hand, the single sheet of stationery, trying to remember.

The Shrine

He would show me, he said, why I must deed over the cobble-stone house to him. As soon as it became legally mine.

He brought me there. He led me inside. He had keys to all the locked places. In my father's study that smelled of mildew and dust a warm autumnal sun fell upon rows of beautifully bound art-books and the golden blank-eyed Buddha on his pedestal. Uncle Jedah was speaking to me in a voice of measured restraint but I could hear the excitement beneath as on a paved bridge you might hear the rush of water invisible beneath.

"Treasure, Merilee! I think you will find it so. 'Truth is beauty, beauty truth.' You have been ignorant for too long, I'm afraid I have indulged you."

Since the special delivery packet of the previous day I had not been able to sit, to lie down, even to remain standing in one place for more than a few minutes. My thoughts were scraps of litter blown in a rushing wind. My heart beat rapidly and lightly as a hummingbird's wings and did not seem to be carrying sufficient oxygen to my brain.

I'd heard Uncle Jedah speak, and I'd seen his mouth move. The glisten of his pearly teeth. But I hadn't seemed to hear what he had said, or had asked me.

The man stood before me massive as a column of some dense, obdurate material. There was a reptilian sheen to his skin, his face remained youthful and unlined, though his eyes, meant to be merry, seemed smaller than I'd remembered, and glassier. Jedah was not much taller than Roosevelt Jimson but must have weighed one hundred pounds more: a flash came to me, as in a child's vision of cartoon terror, of Jedah gripping Jimson in his arms, crushing him as in the coils of a giant python.

"Merilee? Please. Your eyes seem to be open, will you now *see?*"

On the moist, meaty palm of Uncle Jedah's hand were several house keys. Evidently I was to take one of them. Suddenly we were in a game. Jedah was saying that I would have to "discover" which keys fit which locks but that he would guide me of course. It was an accident, I'd chosen a key that fit the several locked drawers in the teakwood desk. "*Voilà!* A good choice, dear. Let's see now what lies inside." Inside the drawers were packets of Polaroid photos. Each was carefully dated: the most recent had been marked, in my father's fastidious hand, *Jan. 1995–Jan. 1999.* I seemed to know beforehand that the contents of the packets would be upsetting for I'd begun to tremble badly, Uncle Jedah had to help steady my hands.

Photos of female bodies, naked. Some were women, and some were girls. Very young girls.

I stared in astonishment. Heat rose into my face, as Uncle Jedah observed me. His look was rapacious, greedy! I could not face that look. I stared at the photographs, the tumble of naked bodies. My impression was of faceless anonymous flesh but of course that was erroneous: each of these individuals had a name, an identity. Pubescent girls with tiny breasts, mature women with large, billowy breasts. Garish lipstick-mouths, in frozen smiles. Pubic hair, and bluntly exposed vaginas from which all pubic hair had been shaved. In one blurred and dreamlike photograph a pasty-pale Caucasian man, naked, headless, was stooping over a young Asian girl who smiled up fearfully at him, her small eyes narrowed as if she expected a blow; the girl could not have been older than ten or eleven, the man was middle-aged, or older, with a sinking potbelly, silver-tipped pubic hairs springing from the pit of the belly, stubby but erect penis gripped in his hand like a rubber sceptor. In another photograph, a mature woman who resembled Alina Jimson was grinning lewdly for the camera as if drunk, or drugged, sprawled on the leather sofa in this very room, thick thighs parted and fingers spreading her labia as if opening her belly in a lurid glistening red wound. The woman's broad-cheeked face was heavily made-up, as I had never seen Alina's face; her breasts bulged and drooped, her stomach fell in fatty creases, varicose veins like lumpy blue worms prominent in her legs and ankles.

Alina, who'd worked for us! Who'd hummed and sang to herself as she vacuumed, scrubbed, scoured; who'd cast me the friendliest, most yearning of smiles, though never forgetting her place in our household as *hired help*.

Lilac's mother . . . Jimson's mother.

I knocked the Polaroid away with a cry of disgust. An entire packet fell to the floor.

Uncle Jimson was amused. "My puritanical niece! Yet you are no sexual novice yourself, are you."

I wanted to protest *But you loved me, I thought! You promised to protect me.*

" 'Taboo' is sentimental nonsense, Merilee. Nature knows no 'taboo' as nature knows no restraint. You are twenty-six, no longer a child. You must understand that your father was a man of the world who enjoyed a secret, one might say a subterranean life, as all men wish to. If there is shame in the air of this room, waves of heat as from a malfunctioning radiator, it is solely in *you*."

Uncle Jedah held out his hand to me another time, that I might select another key. But this time I would not. He laughed at me and went to unlock the closet door, opening it to reveal shelves of art-objects at which I didn't want to look closely. There was also a shelf of videos in black cases, each carefully labeled and dated.

"Simply because you refuse to look, Merilee, doesn't mean that the world does not exist."

I shook my head, refusing.

I shut my eyes, that stung as if I'd been gazing into a bright blinding light.

There remained now unopened in Daddy's study only the lowermost drawer of the filing cabinet. Because he was so stout, Uncle Jedah had difficulty stooping to unlock the drawer. At last, panting, he had to give up. He held out the key at me with a stern look, and like a frightened but willful child I hid my hands behind my back. In disgust Uncle Jedah said, "You see now why your father didn't intend to die so soon. He'd meant to clear away his treasures long before anyone else took possession of the house. If you'd allowed me to take the responsibility of this property from you, Merilee, you'd be spared the silly, sentimental 'shock' you seem now to be experiencing."

This was punishment, then. Uncle Jedah was angry with me, and he was punishing me. I was suffused with shame. I began laughing shrilly. I wanted to clutch at my uncle who towered over me, claw and grab at him, plead for his mercy. I wanted him to console me with a calming touch of his hand in the way of a massive benevolent Buddha but in a swift backhanded gesture as you'd swat away an annoying fly, Uncle Jedah slapped my face hard enough to send me staggering.

"Oh! Oh, but why . . ."

"Sometimes, not often but sometimes female hysteria can be appealing. If set to glorious music properly performed. Otherwise it grates the ears. And an hysterical female face, even an alleged 'pretty' face, stirs revulsion."

The blow had struck the left side of my face. For a moment I thought my cheekbone had been broken. In a daze I fell against the leather sofa. My left ear was ringing. Uncle Jedah was scolding me for having nearly knocked over the "precious, priceless" Tibetan Buddha.

Still I was thinking *He loves me. He wants to protect me.*

"And now, the fruit cellar."

Uncle Jedah dangled a final key before my eyes.

There was no reliable light in the old, earthen-floored part of the cellar. Uncle Jedah fetched a long-handled flashlight from a kitchen closet.

Saying, in a bemused voice, "The old cellar. Where no one ever goes."

We descended the stairs, Uncle Jedah behind me. My face was flaming and both my eyes leaked tears. I was shocked to have been struck in the face but I understood that it was a necessary corrective for I had been behaving childishly. I thought *If I obey Uncle Jedah, if I don't displease him, he will love me again. He will protect me.* Gripping my arm above the elbow, Jedah walked me through the "family room"—that display-room assemblage of low-slung sofa, chairs, TV/DVD/CD console, shag carpet—and into the older part of the cellar where the ceiling was lower, and the moist damp organic-rot odor pinched our nostrils. Jedah switched on the flashlight, illuminating the old, fitted-plank door behind which years ago my mother had crouched to hide. "There is nothing you will see that others have not seen, through the millenia. The ritual of the 'pure sacrifice' is known to all cultures, if sometimes in debased forms as in our own. Of course, you are an American girl of contemporary times. You have been spared too long."

With his foot Uncle Jedah pushed open the door.

I told myself that whatever was revealed to me, I could shut my eyes. I could not be forced to see. A civilian makes a poor witness, Jimson had said.

I was a poor witness! I would take refuge in this fact.

The fruit cellar was farther, still. In a corner of the old cellar where the earthen floor was soft, mucky. In the beam of the flashlight I saw that the door was padlocked.

Padlocked! The door to an old fruit cellar, no longer in use.

"Open it. Here."

Uncle Jedah all but forced the key into my fingers. I fumbled with the padlock, which was covered in grime and cobwebs. My hands were shaking and I couldn't see clearly. Cobwebs like spittle had caught in my eyelashes. The left side of my face throbbed with pain. With a grunt of impatience, Uncle Jedah wrested the key from my hand and opened the padlock himself. He pushed open the door with his foot and nudged me: "Inside, Merilee. *In.*"

I thought *He will trap me in here. I will never leave this place alive.*

A curious lassitude, almost a feeling of peace, came over me.

I would be a witness to my own imprisonment, then. My own punishment which could only be deserved.

Really the fruit cellar was just a large closet, or storage room, in a corner of the old cellar. While I'd lived in the house, no one had ever ventured into it, and no one had given it a thought, so far as I knew. It evoked an era before the 1960s when even comfortably well-off women like my father's mother and grandmother had taken time to preserve fruit in glass jars, an elaborate process requiring many hours of effort; these jars, duly labeled, had been stored in the fruit cellar, a cave-like space hollowed out of the earth and lined with stone and mortar. In the stupefying heat of summer, the fruit cellar would remain cool, even cold. I saw now that a few vestiges of canned fruit remained, on the cobweb-covered wooden shelves. The smell of decay was almost overpowering here. Yet, someone had meant to make the tomb-like space attractive: there was a bas-relief in stone displayed on one of the shelves, very like those pictured in the Hindu temple at Khajurahoe of crudely copulating individuals; and the earthen floor had been dug up, and smoothed over with a rake, covered with layers of delicate white pebbles in a design of simplicity and beauty that brought to mind Zen stone gardens. In the center of the space was a Japanese black-lacquered table shaped like an altar, and on the table were candles in tall brass holders and a carved teakwood box that might have measured three feet by four feet and was eight inches deep. Its lid was fastened shut with a brass clasp. I thought *A child's coffin.*

"Open it."

"Uncle Jedah, no."

"I said open it, Merilee. Obey me."

Uncle Jedah aimed the flashlight beam onto the clasp. With my numbed fingers I tried to do unhook the clasp, but fumbled, and could not. With a snort of disgust, Uncle Jedah handed me the flashlight so that he could work the clasp himself. When he opened the heavy lid, I was surprised to see only just papers, folders, nothing to suggest human remains. Uncle Jedah brought out documents for me to peruse by flashlight: several front pages of the local newspaper featuring photographs of Lilac Jimson and headlines that seemed to me familiar as if I'd seen them only yesterday: 11-YEAR-OLD MT. OLIVE GIRL MISSING. POLICE BAFFLED, NO RANSOM NOTE IN CHILD ABDUCTION. LILAC JIMSON, 11 YEARS OLD. HIGHLANDS PARK, RAVINE AND RIVER BANK SEARCHED. STATE POLICE REPORT "NO LEADS." RESCUE WORKERS SEEK MISSING CHILD, "WE WILL NOT GIVE UP." There was Lilac's smiling face framed in yellow: MISSING 11-YEAR-OLD.

"Oh. God."

I wanted to turn away, but Uncle Jedah held me.

Deeper inside the teakwood box was what appeared to be clothing. A girl's clothing? Soiled green shorts, a pair of lace-edged panties? Red hair ribbons? A swath of dark, crimped hair?

Uncle Jedah said, in a quavering voice, "You may look, Merilee—but not touch. This little shrine, we will brick up forever. As soon as—"

I brought the flashlight down hard on the side of Jedah Graf's head, on his left temple where the bone was soft. The blow came so swiftly and unerringly, Jedah hadn't seen it coming, and could not have protected himself against it if he had. As he staggered, I brought the heavy, long-handled flashlight down another time on his skull, and another time. The force of the blows was so hard, the bones of my hand felt cracked. Uncle Jedah fell heavily, and I threw the flashlight at him, striking the ridge of fatty flesh between his shoulders blades. He whimpered in pain and astonishment. I pushed the black-lacquered box over, on top of him. I ran from the fruit cellar and slammed the door shut.

So quickly! Once I began, I could not be stopped.

I groped for the padlock, secured it back in place and locked it. My heart beat wildly and in elation. "It wasn't Daddy was it! None of this was Daddy! It's *you*."

I ran away then upstairs, and left him. The man's muffled cries as I shut one door after another behind me.

Fading, near-inaudible *Merilee no Merilee help me* and then I wasn't sure that I heard. Beyond the thudding of my own heart, I couldn't hear. More calmly now I proceeded to the front of the house, pausing every few yards to listen. In the cavernous living room where once I'd had to practice piano at the beautiful Steinway, hour after hour, week and month and year after year, I opened the keyboard and struck my fists against the faded ivory keys, fistfuls of chords like nothing that had ever been executed in this house.

"Hate hate *hate you*! Always it was *you!*"

In the marble-floored front lobby, at the heavy oak front door, I paused again to listen. So faint was the sound far away underground, so faint the man's frantic pleas to be released from his dark, earthen-floored dungeon, you could doubt whether you were hearing anything human at all, only just the raucous and intermittent cries of crows at the rear of the Graf property, in the rock-strewn, densely wooded descent to the Highlands Ravine.

The Sentence

He will survive for a long time. He can breathe fouled air, and he can devour spoiled fruit. He can live off his fat. He can call for help, he can beg. He can pray for mercy. He can prevail in his own excrement. For a long time.

Subterranean

Next day I made an appointment with my father's lawyer Mr. Weiden. I saw the shock in the man's face, seeing me. Though I'd bathed in fragrant soapy water as steamy as I could bear, though I'd shampooed and brushed my hair until it shone, though I'd spent forty minutes trying to conceal or at least to mitigate the discolored eye and the wicked bruise that had spread over the left side of my face, I saw the shock in Mr. Weiden's face and chose to ignore it. Before he could speak I explained that I'd made my decision: I would be giving up my inheritance to establish the Dennis Graf Foundation for Public Services, which in turn could endow such worthy organizations as the Disabled Children's Fund and the Graf Scholarships Fund; the property at 299 Lincoln Avenue would be included in the endowment.

For a stunned moment, Mr. Weiden stared at me. My eyes were rimmed in flame but my voice was unwavering. I had to fight the impulse to shield my bruised face as I'd been doing on my way to the law office and so I clasped my hands tightly together in my lap. You could see that I'd made an absolute decision and could not be dissuaded from it.

"But Merilee, have you discussed this with . . ."

"Jedah Graf is no longer executor of my father's estate."

"He—isn't? Since when? What has happened?"

Now Mr. Weiden's shock was complete. He fumbled to remove his glasses, rubbing at his eyes as he continued to stare at me.

I said that I wasn't sure what had happened to trigger my uncle's sudden decision. "He called yesterday to tell me he'd decided to 'embark upon a new career, abroad.' Uncle Jedah has made money on investments, I think. Some of the relatives think that he's long led a double life, a 'subterranean' existence no one in Mt. Olive knows about."

I saw that Mr. Weiden was utterly astonished. Yet in true lawyerly fashion he managed to contain his disequilibrium. Ever the gentleman, he accompanied me through the outer offices of Krampf, Hudgkins, O'Nan & Weiden to the front entrance of the old brownstone building. As he shook my hand in parting he said in a lowered voice, "I'd heard that too, of course. 'The subterranean life of Jedah Graf.' Yes."

The Key

"Not an heiress! No longer."

Jimson came to see me. I'd invited him and he'd been vague about accepting but there he was, parking his car at the curb. I'd been watching for him. I waited for him at the top of the stairs. I knew the man would take one look at my battered face and know immediately what had happened if not the circumstances in which it had happened or its perpetrator. Quickly I embraced him, kissed him on the mouth and pulled him into the apartment so he laughed, "Hey girl!" Inside, the lighting was dim. Hand-dipped candles giving off a fragrant scent had been lighted and positioned strategically. Simmering on the two-burner stove was a large pan of chili made from a recipe I'd found in one of Jedah Graf's cookbooks: dried red kidney beans, ground lean beef, sweet red pepper and onion, garlic, cumin, oregano, coriander, Italian tomatoes and dry red wine and (secret ingredient!) grated unsweetened chocolate. In the refrigerator were two six-packs of Jimson's favorite beer. He'd assumed that we would be going out but I had other plans.

I lifted Jimson's hand, exulting in the warmth and weight of it. While preparing the chili I'd had to sample the dry red wine and felt now a wave of tenderness for Jimson's hand whose palm was lighter-skinned than the back of the hand, a fleshy shade approximately the same as my own. I smiled wondering if the soles of Jimson's feet were this same hue. I thought it was lovely, and funny. If I'd been a fortune-teller I'd have studied the intricate network of lines and creases in the palm, if I'd wanted to be extrascrupulous I might have studied it through the sculpted-glass heart (kept on my windowsill, where it caught the morning sun in a flash of miniature rainbows) but I understood that Roosevelt Jimson who'd been suspicious of the ways of others long before he'd become a cop was regarding me warily. He could see that I was in a mood. He could smell wine on my breath, and God knows what else. He liked me, he liked me fine, he'd liked me more than fine the other evening after we'd left Judge's Bar & Grill, but he wasn't sure of me, what I wanted from him, worse yet what I wanted to give him. A man will shrink from any gift pressed too eagerly upon him, and who can blame him? I wanted badly to kiss Jimson's hand but refrained. Didn't want to scare this man off when I had such better plans for him. Instead I fumbled for the padlock key, in a back pocket of my jeans. My life was so improvised, I hadn't a clear thought what I meant to do until I opened Jimson's hand and placed the key in the palm. "What's this, baby? The key to your heart?" Jimson marveled at me, I was in such a mood. He'd been inside my apartment for less than two minutes and already we were excited and about-to-be-reckless like a couple in a vehicle speeding toward the edge of an escarpment. Neither of us wished to fly over the escarpment, but neither of us wished to be the first to slam on the brakes, either.

"Just something I found, Jimson. And now it's yours."